CROSSROADS

<u>Chapter 1</u>
"Don't drool, it's not healthy," said Tia.

I snapped out of my daze and came back into the real world.

"Sorry," I said.

I was doing it again. Damn... Nicholas Reed, hottest senior, kindest boy, best athlete. I couldn't help but stare. Middle school crushes don't seem to ever go away, do they?

"You know you have no chance right?" Tia said randomly.

I sucked my teeth in annoyance.

"What do you mean?"

"Well, he's you know..."

"Yeah okay Tia, I got it, Nic Reed, #1 popularity rank. Then there is me, Coy Clent probably last in the rank, and not to nice on the eyes."

"Ding Ding Ding," Tia said and chuckled.

I looked at her for a little unable to decide whether to laugh or to shoot her a dead look. But sure enough five seconds later, I burst into laughter as well. (Getting a few odd stares."

We were eating at our regular table in Light View
High School. Nothing was really special about
where we sat. No populars, no high class "rich
girls", just a bunch of low profile losers. This
including myself obviously. We only sat here for
the view. Front row tickets to the "Popular table," as
Tia called it. We sit and watch them every day. The
kids who always had new things, the best cars, and
prettiest faces. Including Nic, and his terrible
girlfriend Harper Faharo.

It was time, they came inside the lunchroom. The
best part about sitting here was the view. And the
worst part was the view.

Nic and Harper approached the table, Jonas at their
back, along with Kingsley, my best friend.

"Hey Coin," Harper said with a smirk on her face.

"Oh, hey Herpes! How's your rash treating you? My
mom (her pharmacist) told me you had to increase
your dose, cause it got gasp shockingly worse."

Everyone burst into laughter. I hung my head proud,
turned to Nic and winked.

Wait... What did I just do?

Nic gave me an odd look and walked away, which
by that time Harper had sat down at their table and
began throwing her daily fit.

Tia and I sat and ate for a little while more, watching the "Popular kids" till the bell rang.

Tia and I began walking to our last classes. Mine, chemistry, her's art. She was always so damn lucky.

"Hey girl!" I heard from behind me. Kingsley.

I rolled my eyes and turned around, "What do you want Kingsley?"

"Why so rude this morning? Did Harper get your panties in a twist or are you just angry that your hubby still hasn't noticed you?"

I sighed and looked at the floor.

"You know I could just tell him for you Coy. It's not that hard." He let out a chuckle.

Kingsley doesn't understand, and he never will. He likes boys and he's a boy. So nothing really phases him because to him, there are many fish in the sea.

"No," I said heated.

"Okay pepper, well you better get on your way to chem, Mrs. Bristol will write you up if you're late."

"Jeez, It's true! Thanks, Kingsley," I said as I ran down the hall books in han-

thud

My books fell and I was on the floor. I looked in front of me and saw... Oh no. Nicholas Reed. I. My. Front. On the floor. Because. Of me.

"I'm so sorry," I said hesitantly.

"It's okay," he laughed.

I loved his laugh, it was like music to my ears.

"You're Coi-"

"Coy," I said.

"Oh, sorry, Harper always says Coin," he said as he laughed.

"Yeah, she kinda has it out for me."

We both laughed. I stood there for a while, staring, admiring, drooling (not really), till the sound of the bell shattered my thoughts.

"Oh lord," I said as I picked up my books.

He helped too.

"Thanks!," I shouted and dashed down the hall searching for room 202 for Chemistry.

"Nice to meet you Coi-, I mean Coy," He laughed again and cruised down the hall.

A huge smile spread across my face. I ran up the stairs, down next hall and finally into class 202.

Chapter 2

Surprise, surprise. I walk into my class just in time. But, I am greeted with an unpleasant sight. A blonde-haired, blue-eyed, tan-skinned, 5'4 girl. Harper. A devious smile creeps across her face.

"Hey Coin," she says as I see myself fall to the floor.

She tripped me, on the first day of my senior year. I am literally shamed.

A boy points directly at me and yells "Dumbass". The whole class burst into laughter and my face burned red. I stand up and dust off my clothes. When I get my balance I turn and look Harper right in the eyes. As I open my mouth Mrs. Bristol walks into the room.

"Settle down students, we don't need a brawl on the first day of school," she stated as she gave me the stink eye.

Harper twirled her long, curly, blonde hair in her fingers and proceeded to her seat near the open window. She sat next to the window every year because it was so-called "good for the pores."

I was walking around the class looking for a seat (but as it happens I have really bad luck) the only place I saw to sit was next to Harper.

I hung up my bag and took my seat, as I sat down something flew into my hair. Gum. I yanked it out and threw it back to the sender, trying to listen to what we'd be learning about, safety drills, and all that other jazz they teach on the first day of school.

After a head-bobbing, boring, 40 minutes class was finally over.

I grabbed my galaxy patterned cheeseburger Jansport backpack and headed to my locker. I opened it up with my simple code 30-0-30, grabbed my books, filled my bag, and left the front door of the school.

"Nicholas!" I heard two people shout. I turned around to get my last glimpse of him for the day, but was saddened when it was just Tia and Kingsley.

"Why'd you guys do me like that?" I said pouting.

They began laughing hysterically.

"Sorry we had to," Tia said, still continuing to laugh.

"I talked to Nicholas after this period and he said he finally talked to you, he sounded really happy and said you were beautiful," said Kingsley.

"Oh my god, really?" I blurted out.

"No, but he said you bumped into him today and it was a pleasure meeting you." Kingsley smiled largely, holding in a laugh, but no need, because Tia let out her own.

"Well that's a start," Tia said.

We all began laughing.

"All we need to do now is help out your dull appearance, get Harper out of the way, and Nic will be all your!" Tia said sarcastically.

Our laughter loudened, my stomach ached, and my head lightened.

I inhaled deeply and let it out.

"Thanks for the laugh," I said.

"Today has been horrible," Tia said.

"As if you know girl," Kingsley shouted.

We all giggled for a few more seconds. We kept chatting for a few more minutes until I saw my mothers car pull up.

"Bye Ti, Bye K!" I shouted as I ran towards my mom's black 2017 jeep.

"Bye!" They both shouted back. I hopped into the car and we drove off.

A few minutes of silence went by, 1, 2, 3, 4, and then my mom finally said something.

"So how was your first day? Any crushes besides that Mick, me, Micleass?"

"Mom, it was okay, but it's Nicholas and no. And plus, who said I even liked him anyway, because I don't."

"Well, your browser history says otherwise."

I gasp.

"Mom! Why are you reading my browser history?" I shout.

"It's a family computer, not private property Coy," she laughs.

Ugh.

We pull into the garage. I open the car door and jump out, open the house door, and drop my bag on the table. I take off my white converse, place them in my hand and walk to the fridge. I open it up and look around.

Salad? No. Mashed potatoes? No. Chicken nuggets? No. Cheeseburgers and fries? Yes!

I place it out on the place nearby and warm it up for the 30 seconds.

Beep beep beep.

I remove my food from the microwave, the smell filling the air. I walk into my room, place my page on the table, and lick the door. I walk over to the mirror and take a long hard look at myself.

Brown hair, green eyes, light tan color, 5'4. So what's so bad about me? What's so different between Harper and me? Then there is Nic. Dirty blonde hair, amber eyes, 6'0, beautiful complexion, mesmerizing face.

If it were my decision, I'd choose me. After all, amber and green would make beautiful eye colors for our future children.

I let out a long, deep sigh and move away from the mirror. I grab my food and open my computer, going to YouTube.

"How to get your crush to notice you," I type into the search bar. I click on the first video. It's a blonde-haired Hawaiian looking girl. I think she said her name is Eva?

I start listening, at the same time I'm taking notes.

I finish the video and then my phone goes off.

Ding ding ding.

I pick it up.

"Tia! I've figured it out. I've got it!"

<u>Chapter 3</u>

Kinda left you hanging there, sorry.

Today is the 2nd week of school, so Tia and I are going to put my plan to action today. We call it "Almanglo." I really don't know how we came up with such an odd name. Anyways this is what we have planned:

Get Nic "Almanglo"

1. Go to Clever Mall and buy a new wardrobe.

2. Go to Sephora and Ulta and buy makeup.

3. Go to the hair salon and get hair done (obviously.)

4. Get nails done at that dumb nail place

5. Go grocery shopping

Ignore that last one..... Hahaha

I throw on my backpack and walk to school. When I got there I saw Tia waiting at the front door.

"Finally," she said.

We hid our backpacks behind a big bush and ran to distance ourselves from the school. About a mile and a half later (We used to do track) we finished running, as we figured we were far enough from the school.

"Let's walk now," I said taking a breath in between each word.

"Walk? Haha! I only stopped here because I called an Uber. Did you really think we were going to walk for 30 some minutes to the mall? And on top of that, shop while we're sweaty?"

"Uh, no." I stuttered.

"Yeah, right..." Tia said rolling her eyes.

5 minutes later, our driver, "Craig" (fishy name, I know) pulled up in his black 2016 Audi.

"Are you, um, Tia," he said as he checked his phone.

"Yes, Craig?" Tia said.

"Yes ma'am, y'all can hop in the back seats," he said, me just hearing his southern accent.

He unlocked the door and Tia and I went inside.

30ish minutes went by without and utter from anyone. Tia and I sat in the back texting each other, rather than speaking.

"Well, we have arrived," Craig said as he switched the car into park.

"Thanks," I mummer and hopped out of the comfy car. 5 seconds later he drove off in a flash.

I looked around to take in my surroundings, unable to figure out what to do first.

"What do you want to do first?" Tia shouted in excitement.

"Well, honestly I don't know, maybe we should just try and see-"

"Okay, clothes it is!"

I smiled as Tia grabbed my hand and dragged me into the mall, and to the nearest clothing shop. 'Forever 21' I read as I was being dragged into the store. If I must admit, I've actually never been to the mall. Only Walmart, Ross, and occasionally, that overrated red place you people call Target.

I look around the store and see many things. Crop tops, jeans, leggings, graphic tees, shit I'd wear if I went to the gym, and more. I go over to the graphic tees first but am quickly dragged away by Tia.

"No!" she quietly yelled.

"You're no longer a child, you're 17. No more 'Ugh Monday' and 'Fries Before Guys' tees, leave it to the freshmen."

I laughed louder than need to. I thought it was funny. The people around us, not so much. I straightened my face and proceeded to the crop tops. Tia began taking out many tops and after she had about 50, she gave them to me saying "Go try them."

I went into the dressing room with 42 tops and came out with 20. It wasn't that bad. I liked my choices, I was confident. I showed them to Tia and after a few "Oohs" and "Ahhs," we headed to check out.

When we got to the front of the line, I put the tops, jeans, and a few pairs of leggings Tia had chosen for me on the counter.

"324.92," the cashier said after she rang everything up.

"Whoa, Tia, I don't have that ty-" She cut me off like usual.

"Here you go," Tia said to the cashier as she held out her credit card.

Damn, I forgot Tia was rich. Billionaire father, gold-digging mama (no offense, she even says it).

"Here you go," the cashier said as tore the printed receipt, put it in the bag, and handed it to Tia along with her credit card.

I am honestly so lucky to have Tia. Beautiful, brown-haired, blue-eyed, rich best friend.

After visiting 6 more shops for clothes, 2 for makeup, 3 for shoes, and the nail salon, we were finally at coming to our last stop... The hair salon.

We entered the hair salon named 'Bad and Boujee Salon.' We were greeted by what seemed to be a french male.

"Tiaa!' he shouted.

"Armando!" They hugged like old-time friends in The Vampire Diaries.

"Come, come, come! Let me fix your hair, even though it is already beautiful!" he said.

"Great, but it's not for me, it's for my friend here, Coy."

"Oh.," Armando said as he pulled closer and began touching my hair.

"Just dreadful," he said loudly.

<u>Chapter 4</u>

I had done it; we had done it. Tia and I had made my dreams come to reality. The hairdresser did a terrific job, he was really rude, but did great.

My hair now had volume. A shiny brown at the top which now faded into a warm golden tone. He had curled it to perfection and restored its life, plus added moisture.

I got a beautiful coffin-shaped full set with those powdered acrylic things. It was painted a soft Bambi brown.

Last of all, my makeup, 3 bags of concealers, foundation, eyeshadow, highlighter, lip gloss, and a bunch of other things that I really did not know the name of. Since I had bought so much, the sweet employees showed me how to do my makeup.

Everything was ready, now all I had to do was put my plan into action.

Now Nic would drool over me, rather than the opposite way around.

I put my hair into a net provided by Armando and got ready to sleep. In only a few minutes, I was knocked out. No sign of life probably, I was physically, and mentally drained.

In what seemed like 40 minutes, but in reality 7 hours and 24 minutes, my alarm clock was ringing, indicating it was time to get ready for school.

I sat up and hit the snooze button forcefully. I picked up my phone and began scrolling through Instagram.

What a delightful say for school, typed one perky cheerleader in her caption. *Fuck it, I'm ditching,* another typed as he showed himself at target.

I let out a sigh.

I hopped off my bed and hopped into the shower, making sure not a droplet of water touched my head. 12 minutes later I get out and began putting on my new clothes.

"Graphic Tee?" I questioned myself.

"Nah, Tia would be disappointed," I said two seconds later.

I picked up a maroon-colored lace-up crop top. I then grabbed a light-colored denim jean along with my Jordans.

"Perfect," I shouted with enthusiasm.

Chapter 5

I walked into school at around 7:00 am, which was 15 minutes before classes would start. My hair curled to perfection, nails on fleek, (that is what they call it nowadays, right?) and clothes on point.

As I walked in the hallways, eyes met my whole body from every direction.

They were staring.

My confidence boosted by the second. I continued walking down the halls, adding a bit more hip to my walk.

"Is she new," I heard someone say.

"Probably,' said another.

"Wow, she's… hot," I heard a familiar voice say.

I looked to the direction the voice had come from.

Harper.

She thought I looked… hot?

A smile crept onto my face as I continued walking to my locker, #324.

I put my passcode in, 30-0-50.

As I twist the stroll to open it, I feel a tap on my shoulder, and begin to smell a nice scent; a familiar one.

Oh my god... Nic.

I turned around slowly and took a deep breath.

Chapter 6

"Hey Coy…" Nic said as he scratched the back of his neck.

"Hey, um, what's up?" I said realizing I sounded like an absolute idiot.

He laughed.

There it goes again.

"I like this change you're trying out," he smiled.

My cheeks burned in the color red.

"Uh, thanks, I actually-" I was cut off (thank god) by the voice of a hyperactive teen; Harper.

She hugged Nic tightly and pecked him on the cheek. He turned to his side and squeezed her hand. I saw it clearly. In her eyes, love, and in his eyes, lust.

He turned back his attention to me, and as he opened his mouth to speak, a louder voice from his side spoke up.

"Hi, I'm Harper," she held out her hand smiling like a two-faced bitch (well maybe to me it seemed that way). Harper looked down at my hand, gesturing that I should shake hers.

God, do I look that different?

I ignored her hand.

Nic turned to her and whispered in her ear lightly. She took a large step back, her smile faded, and her eyes widened.

"COIN?" She shouted a little too loudly.

"It's you?" She paused, her face puzzled.

"Whoever did this to you is a true miracle worker." She laughed.

Nic next to her still as a wall. She tapped his shoulder and he let out an artificial laugh.

Harper and I have been enemies since the first grade, so I assumed and am continuing to assume that it is a lifelong hatred.

She focused her attention in 5 seconds, seizing her laugh.

"Well I guess we could give this friendship thing a shot." She sighed, "Friends?" a faint smile on her face.

I burst into laughter, spat on here shoe, closed my locker, and walked off.

Lol, if only that were possible.

I stook out my hand returning the "friends"
statement.

She smiled, grabbed my hand, and dragged me
down the hallway.

"Nic, close her locker, bye! Remember to tell Saf
that I won't make it to cheer practice when you go
for football!"

"Okay, bye!" He shouted back.

As we walked down the hall, I saw Tia.

"TIA!" I shouted.

She turned her neck so fast, I'm surprised it didn't
break. She fixed her bag and ran towards me.
Realizing the person next to me, she slowed down.
She now was approaching very slowly.

"Hey?"

"Hey!" Harper said back enthusiastically. "We are
friends now. IF you would like to join us at the
Japena Carnival later today, we would be pleased to
have you."

Harper moved close to Tia, releasing my arm once
and for all.

She bent over and whispered in her ear, "Good job, I didn't have the guts to do it. And now that you have.." she looked over at me, "it's for the better."

I rolled my eyes lightly, hoping she did not see.

Harper backed away from Tia and grabbed her and me by the arms.

"We are going to be great friends. Tia you are rich, Coy is pretty, and I am both."

We all laughed (me at her stupidity, Tia as well, but her, she thought she was funny).

Ding

The bell sounded loud. I unlatched myself from Harper and smiled at both her and Tia.

"See you guys after school," I said as I began walking to my first class, Spanish.

"Don't forget! My house, 6, nice red or blue clothing. The carnival is covered, I am paying!" Harper shouted.

"Okay, bye!" I shouted back.

She and Tia walked off into the same direction. Going into their first classes, Tia, art, and Harper, Orchestra.

<u>Chapter 7</u>

I looked at the clock.

5:36pm.

In 24 minutes, I'd have to go to Harper Fahara's house to attend a carnival with both her and her friends. Who were now, supposedly, my friends.

I called up Tia.

"Hello" she said sounding nervous.

"What's wrong?" I said.

"Nothing, just a bit worried about this thing with Harper."

"Me too!" We both laughed.

"I've chosen my outfit… It's blue." Tia stated, now sounding confident.

"Oh-" I paused, "I'm going to go red, I just need to pick it out."

I heard someone shout Tia in the background.

"Yes," Tia shouted, "Coy, I'm sorry. I gotta go, see you at 7."

"6!" I shouted.

"6, yeah right, thanks, bye." she cut the phone.

I walked over to my closet and looked through my jeans. I chose a dark denim short with cuts on the fronts.

"Shirt, shirt, shirt," I said continuously looking through my tops.

I spotted a red crop top, it cut off in the corners, and it was long sleeve. It was cute.

I got a velvet choker out of my jewelry box. I put on my clothes quickly and entered the bathroom. My curling iron was already plugged in, so I began combing through my hair.

I opened the drawer in the bathroom and brought out a bigger curling barrel to replace the one on the counter.

I placed it in and began curling my hair (Lana Del Rey style).

When I finished, I placed the curling iron back on the counter, and unplugged the tool. After spraying my hair with hairspray, I walked back into my room, getting a glimpse of the clock.

5:52pm.

I screamed loudly, surprisingly the neighbors didn't call the police.

I ran downstairs to where my shoes were, Nike Air Forces, in white, not black. People who wear black ones truly do not care about their lives. I put them on, grabbed my car key, and went to my car.

Harper's house was on W Washington Rd, which was 5 minutes away, but it was 5:56.

I drove 7 mph over the speed limit (rebellious, I know) trying to get there in time.

A red light got in my way. *Oh fuck.* I was at the light for a good two minutes. The lighted flashed green, but the person in front of me was a teen texting their life away.

I honked my horn, which was a bit rude of me, but rough circumstances call for desperate measures. The girl turned around, gave me the stink eye, and continued to text as if it were an assignment.

I sped up.

Gilmore, Decatur, YES! Washington Rd.

I turned onto the street a little too fast causing the wheels to screech along the streets.

I drove into Harper's driveway. Tia's car was already there, a stunning G Wagon with the license plate 'PRNCESS,' I looked at it and smiled.

I got out of my car, and walked up to Harper's front door wiping the streak of swear daring to drip down from my forehead. Before I even was able to bring myself to knock on the door, Harper opened it up, standing there with her arms crossed over her chest.

"You're late," she said gloomily.

"It's 6:03!" I said in a panic.

"I had to run out of my house, and I was speeding. I could have of been on ti-" She stopped me.

"It's okay, I'm not that crazy," she said smiling.

I faintly smiled back. She moved to the side, opening her door wider, inviting me inside.

I walked inside and was astonished. Her loft was bigger than my whole house. Chandeliers hanging from the towering ceilings.

Many large glass windows in the building showing amazing views of the whole California.

"Wow," I said in my head.

"What?" Harper said.

I guess I said that aloud.

"Nothing, my foot was just feeling a bit odd, it's probably because of all my running."

"Right…" Harper said doubtfully.

Tia came out from the corner behind the steps.
Thank God.

"Hey Coy," she said, "Isn't her house amazing? It's said it was the house used in Mean Girls for Regina George."

"It is!" Harper said, "Cost quite a few millions, but my parents did not mind. Anything for me, right?

Yeah, except for them. I thought to myself.

We all stood there awkwardly for a good two minutes.

"Shall we get going?" Harper said, finally breaking the silence.

"Yeah," I said laughing, Tia joining along.

Harper led us into her garage of cars. It was full of Lamborghinis, Ferraris, G Wagons, BMWs, Soccer mom vans, and much more. She took a key from the side of the door, it being the big 7 seater Jeep in the back.

Tia and I looked at Harper oddly and looked at each other in the next second.

"What?" Harper said with a puzzled look on her
face, "I have other friends coming as well."

We shrugged and followed Harper into the car. She
put in the key and twisted it to the right. She put the
car in reverse, opened the garage, and we drove off.

<u>Chapter 8</u>

We reached the carnival. Bursts of lights coming from all directions.

A big Ferris wheel to my left and a scary-looking roller coaster to my right. My eyes opened wide at the sight of the 'Popular Group' members running over to us. All of them dressed in red, blue, or white. They looked like an American flag,

They finally reached us, after what seemed to be forever. Were they walking in slow motion or what? Anyways, a blonde-headed, brown-eyed girl named 'Saf' hugged me.

"Hi, my name is Saf!" as she pulled out of the hug.

"When did you move to LVHS?" She said boldly.

She really said it with her whole chest. I could not tell if she was being serious or joking.

"Oh, I've been here since freshman year," I said giggling.

She laughed back, squinted her eyes, and tilted her head a bit. She thought I was joking, but I just ignored it.

Nic emerged from the crown and my stomach dropped.

"Hey Tia, uh, Hey Coy," He said with uncertainty.

"Hey," Tia and I both said, me holding myself back from blushing.

"Let's go to the Ferris Wheel guys!" a boy shouted from the crowd (it was probably Jonas).

Everyone just shouted a simple 'yeah' and made their way to the ride.

The conductor asked us for our wristbands. Harper brought out a stack of cash and handed it to the conductor.

"14 wristbands please!" She said smiling deviously.

He handed them to her and we all put ours on.

"Enjoy the ride!" The conductor said counting the hundreds of dollar change Harper had just given him.

They all began choosing people to sit with while Harper latched onto Tia, so I was alone. I looked around for Saf, but she was partnered up with a girl named Kadence. The only person left was Nic.

Great!

I just concluded I was going myself.

"Nic, go with Coy!" Harper shouted.

My eyes widened, I quickly forced them closed, and opened them back up less wide.

Nic put his hand on the back of his neck and strolled over slowly. A faint smile on his face.

"Let's go everybody," Saf said in her commanding cheerleader voice.

Everybody went on the ride two by two with their designated partners. It was Nic and I's turn. We got on the ride, the conductor closed the entrance to the hot air balloon like seat we were in, and the ride began.

"So, uh, how is Buddy?"

"He died a few years back," I said.

Buddy was my dog. Nic lived on my street when we were younger. He was the chubby short boy back then. Braces on his teeth, and those type of sandals that would make you question his livelihood.

"Why did you decide to um…"

"Change?" I said boldly.

"Yeah.." He said scratching his brow.

"I felt like I needed a change. Senior year, well, it needed some changes. I wanted to meet new people, but I just wasn't in the same category as 'em, you know?"

God, I said too much.

He chuckled lightly.

"I know, remember, short, fat, brace face me?" He paused, "You've always been beautiful Coy. There are no categories. Everyone is the same. If you wanted to speak to me, I am available." He gave me a sincere smile. One I hadn't seen since we were kids.

"Thank you," I said.

He looked into my eyes, me looking back. A glimpse of something sparked in his eyes. What was it? He began leaning in… I felt my face turn bloodshot red.

I turned my face right, and pretended to admire the city I'd lived in my whole lifetime.

"I'm sorry," he said shamefully.

"It's… okay." I said faintly.

The ride stopped, and we finally got off along with everybody else, two by two.

I spotted Tia and pulled her to the side. I was breathing in and out heavily, but at the same time trying to scream.

"What the fuck is it now?" Tia said, "Why is your face red? Did he hurt you?" Her face scrunched.

"No… but he, um, almost…" I couldn't go on.

Tia gasped.

I turned a few heads, but luckily not Harpers.

How would Harper react if she found out, this would make her 1000x worse than she ever was to me before.

"It's okay, I got you." Tia was approaching Nic.

I ran up and stopped her just in time.

"No!" I said shouting but whispering at the same time, "Leave it, it was just a mistake. It doesn't take single day for someone to begin liking another. He was just blind for a second, but he came back to his senses, he even apologized."

"Okay, but Harper is our friend now, so if we, or you, want to maintain that, just remember that the next time you're with HER boyfriend." Tia stomped off.

Why was she angry? How fast can a group of unappreciative spoiled children change a sincere person under twenty-four hours.

I thought back to middle school. Tia was a 'rich popular girl.' I was that one shy unnoticed girl.

One of the cool boys thought it would be fun to start bullying me.

From shoves in the hall, to texts, to full-on fists coming from left and right at me.

Tia saw it one day when I was at the school bus stop.
She kicked the boy in his stomach so hard his food came back up. Since that day, we've been best friends.

As our friendship grew, her popularity dropped.

She gave it all up for me. A bullied mid-class girl with no sense of responsibility.

I've been holding her back. Now it was her chance to get back up to the top again, but… As always, I was holding her back.

I looked off and saw Tia eating cotton candy with Harper, a girl named Carly, and Ren.

She looked happy. She wasn't alone. Her hair flowing, blue cropped hipster shirt on with her American skirt.

She descrved to be here. She honestly deserved all these friends and people around her. On the other hand, I didn't deserve any of it. The clothes, the fun, the friends, nothing.

I yanked off my wristband and threw in the trash. I bought a Mountain Dew and a bag of Takis and left the carnival. Nic saw me, but kept away. I took off my shoes, and walked home.

<u>Chapter 9</u>

It was Saturday morning. I picked up my phone and checked for anything.

24 text messages from Tia.

"Where are you?"

"I'm sorry!"

"How did you get home?"

"Are you home?"

"Please message me back."

"Hope you are okay."

The list went on.

7 missed calls from Nic, Harper, and Tia.

Wait. Backtrack. Nic?

How did he get my number? I took another look at Tia's texts.

"I gave Nic your number. I'm sorry, I thought maybe he would be able to reach you because you were angry at me."

I threw my phone to the left side of my bed and got up.

I was still in my clothes from last night. I slipped off of them and replaced it with my black Adidas joggers and white halter top.

I put on socks which didn't match because I obviously didn't have time to find the matching pair.

I hopped down the stairs while tying my hair into a bun. I opened the fridge and grabbed oats, acai, milk, and berries. I went into the cabinet in the kitchen and grabbed a bowl.

I was feeling spontaneous today.

I grabbed a spoon and rinsed it in the sink. I then brought the bowl and spoon over on the island in the middle of the kitchen.

I poured in the vanilla milk first, followed by the ats, acai, and the berries.

I've never actually made this before. I saw it on youtube and felt like giving it a try.

I put my plate on the eating table and poured myself a glass of orange juice. I sat down and took a bite of my food.

Mmmm.

This shit lowkey smacks. I began rushing my food down. I took sips of the juice and continued eating it. I took a break to get my phone. It just didn't feel natural eating and not checking my Snapchat or Instagram feed.

I got it off my bed and put my phone on Do Not Disturb mode. *Thank iPhone for making this feature.*

I walked back into the kitchen and finished the rest of my food. I drank down my drink and as I went to put my dishes in the sink a loud knock on the door frightened me, causing the plates to fall and shatter.

"OH FUCK!" I shouted loudly.

I kicked the pieced to the side with my foot, being cautious not to cut my foot.

I walked to the door, opened it up, and there was Saf.

"Hey," she said stepping inside my house… she was texting.

"What's up?" I said.

She looked up from her phone and put a finger up to indicate 'hold on.'

I rolled my eyes. *What a drama queen.*

She looked up after a good 4 minutes.

"Harp and Ti sent me to get you," she started chewing gum.

"Ti? Harp?"

"Yeah, Tia, and Harper," she said in a duh type of way.

"Well as you can see, it's Saturday. I just want to stay in and watch Netflix and eat food," I said.

"They feared that, but it's okay Coco."

"Coco? What? Huh?"
Saf walked to the door as she sent a text message. She opened it up, and running through the door was Harper and Tia, or should I say 'Harp' and 'Titi' lol.

They ran to me, hugging me tightly. Tia pulled out and Harper followed.

"If you're staying in, we are too," Tia said, me now just noticing they were in pajamas.

"What? No." I paused, "Please, I want to be alone today. I already feel bad enough for what happened last night. I'm just glad Ni-" I slipped up.

"Nic did what?" Harper's face turned serious, her expressions angry.

"Oh my god," said Tia.

<u>Chapter 10</u>
"Nic did WHAT?" Harper repeated louder this time.

I messed up, I was done for. If Kingsley were here, he would be able to change the subject or make up a truly believable lie.

"Nic almost kissed her. He leaned in, she backed away." Tia said nervously.

Harper's face turned pure red, then purple, and back to red. Her eyes filled with tears, about to overflow and fall out from the obstacle holding it.

"It's not true, he'd never! It's you who did it. You leaned in, not him! He looked away, not you! I can't believe I was actually beginning to li-" she burst into tears.

My heart ached. I could see the same look on Tia's face.

Saf looked up from her phone.

"It's true," she said boldly, "It's all over Instagram, a gif of Coy Clent dodging from the Nic Reed on a Ferris Wheel.

Saf turned her phone to us, and the room was filled with gasps and more sobs from Harper.

"Oh dear," Tia and I said at the same time.

<u>Chapter 11</u>

It was Sunday afternoon, the weather was a cool 65 degrees, and a whole group of us planned to go to Disneyland.

I begged Kingsley to come and he finally agreed.

I straightened my hair with a little curl at the ends. I put on black shorts with tears in the front (my go-to). I put a red crop top on, and lastly my cute Minnie ear headband. Courtesy of Harper of course.

We'd all leave our homes at 3:00pm on the dot, and then we'd meet up in the parking lot where the bus would carry us to the main park.

It was currently 2:43pm. I was already done, the last thing I put on was my white vans.

I hopped down the steps and grabbed a croissant burger out of the fridge, I warmed it up and began to eat, of course paying attention to the time.

I looked at the clock.

2:58.

My heart pounded faster. After the other day, I don't know what's going to happen between Nic and I.

Harper forgave me after she saw the video. She gave me a hug, wiped her tears, and asked, "Who has ice cream," with a small smile on her face.

She was less bitchy and really sweet when you knew her. That change of mine actually made my senior year better.

The time was 2:59. I grabbed my cute shoulder bag given to me by Sad, slid my phone inside, and left the house through the garage doors.

I opened my car door, sat down, and turned the key,

I closed the door, put the car in reverse, and drove off.

I left exactly at 3:00. I felt very proud! Disneyland was only a good 10 minutes away from my house, but somehow I made it in 8.

I got to the parking lot. There was a boarder type looking place where you pay for parking space.

I paid the fee and collected my receipt so I'd be able to leave.

The man lifted up the line thing blocking me from entering the parking lot. As soon as it lifted, I pulled up to a great parking space near the bus stop.

I got out of my car and looked around for all of my friends.

"There they are," I whispered to myself.

They were in the line of the bus stop.

All the girls wore some type of red and Minnie ears, it was really cure. All the boys dressed like, well boys.

I spotted Nic in the front of the line and avoided all eye contact. He and Harper were holding hands, which was a very good sign.

"Aye, everybody, Coy is here!" a nice boy named Grant said.

Everyone's eyes darted towards me, some said 'Hi' and others said 'Hey.'

Nic was the last to look. His eyes met my eyes.

Oh god, after all that avoidance.

He turned away fast making sure Harper didn't see I took a deep breath.

"So far, so good," I mumbled to myself.

The bus came down the road. Everybody entered one by one. I took my seat in the back far away from Nic and Harper.

Kingsley! He came into the bus and walked towards me. He handed me a bag of snickers (best friends were made for this) and sat down next to me.

"Hey girl, I came," Kingsley said laughing.

"I can see that," I laughed as well.

The bus left the parking lot. Everywhere around us was filled with palm trees and beautiful people.

"Wow, I've never been here before," I said.

"You're odd Coy," He laughed, "Who had never been to Disneyland?"

"Me," I said as I crossed my arms in a jokingly manner.
We both laughed.

The bus finally stopped. I got up along with everybody in the bus.

"Thanks for the chocolates!" I told Kingsley, holding up the bag of snickers.

"No problem, I know it's your favorite candy. But it's not just for you, I'm feeling chocolatey too."

"Okay sir," I said eating a snicker.

Kingsley put his hand inside the bad and grabbed one himself.

He threw the chocolate on the bus and we exited the bus.

Our whole group gathered and we began walking to the place where you purchase a ticket.

"Fast pass or regular," The man at the desk asked.

"Fast pass," we all said.

We all passed one by one, each paying for ourselves.

When we walked in there was a bunch of plants, followed by a bathroom, after the bathrooms, you got the small shops.

All of us continued walking until we reached the parade. It was quite enjoyable.

There were many Disney princesses and princes. Ariel, Moana, Else, etc.

The parade finished about 30 minutes later and we all decided to go on a few rides.

"First, the Pirates!" I shouted and everyone cheered as they rushed toward the direction of the ride.

When we got there we entered the FastPass line and began walking down.

After a bit, we finally reached where the conductor
was stationed.

"How many?" the Disneyland employee said
sticking out his hand in front of the skinny brown-
headed regular pass boy, indicating stop.

"We are 8," Harper said, as she looked around and
recounted all of us.

Saf, Kingsley, Me, Harper, Tia, Nic, Grant, and
Cleo.
I let out a sigh of relief knowing I wouldn't get left-
back.

The employee directed us toward the little boat.

Saf and Harper sat in the front, Kingsley and Grant
in the second row, then Nic and … *oh shit.*

I got into the seat and Nic followed behind. As the
boat began to move, everywhere got darker. I was
getting scared, but chose to play it off.

I was next to Nic, not Kingsley, so I had to suck up
my fears and keep quiet. I shifted closer to the edge
of the boat seat, and nearer to the water.

Nic noticed.

Lights flashed, pirates moved about, birds sang, it
was amazing.

I began getting so dark, I feared something would
come out of the water.

I shifted back into the dear, turned my head the
opposite direction of Nic, and placed my hand on
the space next to me.

I wanted to take a picture but they had announced
no photography allowed.

"Kingsley," I whispered, trying to get his attention.

No luck.

I could barely see the people in front of me by this
point. I decided to let my anxiety go and just enjoy
the ride. I sat fully back, and sat as if I were with a
good friend. Not tense, not too close, just normal.

I felt a hand over my shoulder and another grabbing
my hand in the space between Nic and me.

I closed my eyes and took a large gulp. I pushed his
hand off my shoulder and moved to the edge of the
seat.

<u>Chapter 12</u>

Monday morning and I couldn't, well, didn't want to go to school.

Disneyland was great, but a killer on the feet. I don't know what, or better question how, I am going to avoid Nic or get him to stop.

Don't get me wrong, I've wanted his attention for a long, long, long time. But when he is with Harper? No thanks. I'd also rather not want to ruin my friendship with all these amazing people I've met. Saf, Cleo, Grant, is Jonas. God, it would hurt.

Buzz. Buzz. Buzz.

I looked over my shoulder and saw my phone ringing.

Harper.

My heart began pounding.

"Oh shit," I shouted kick in the side of my bed.

I picked up the phone letting out a long and deep sigh.

I answered-

"Hello," I said in the fakest, most perky voice of the century.

"Hey! Why aren't you at school? I have a-," I cut her off.

"Harp, I'm sick," I said faking a cough.

"Oh my god. Don't worry, after school, I'll bring you my organi-,"

"Harper," I said.

"What?"

"Harper!"

"What?"

"It's okay. You're a great friend to me, but I truly would just love to be alone. Plus, I don't have an appetite, and I don't want to waste a good meal," I said in a way that made my nose sound stuffy.

"Oh... well, sorry, feel better. See you when you come back," Harper said gloomily, cutting the phone.

I exited the phone app on my phone and went onto Instagram.

I opened it to the navigation page and type in an N.

Immediately his page popped up.

I scrolled through this feed on Instagram and noticed something truly odd.

ALL the pictures of him and Harper has been deleted. His bio still said taken though?

I scrolled up and refreshed his page.

A NEW POST.

It was a picture. He was in surfer wear. Hair drenched to the side by water. His eyes glowing in the sun, and a surfboard in his left hand.

I scrolled down a little further to get a view of his caption.

As I began reading his caption, my heart fastened, my hands began to sweat, and my mouth became dry.

"People you've never noticed. They come into your life and make you question life. They come in when you need them. They make you question yourself. They even make you love again. My heart had been stolen, and now I've been awoken."

I refreshed his picture two more times to see if he would change the caption.

Nope.

I referenced a third time, but this time a comment appeared.

It was Harper.

"Oh my god! I love you! Why didn't you come to school? Oh you're surfing! Call me! Xoxo, Harper," she typed.

I refreshed a last time. More comments flooded in and I decided to look at them.

I scrolled all the way to the top to view Harper's comment again.

It was gone.

I left the comment section and refreshed the picture one last time.

Harper has commenters again, but not a lovey-dovey comment.. a kinda confused, angry one.

"..."

My heart paused, causing me to choke.

I placed my phone down on the table and took deep, long breaths.

What am I going to go?

I pulled my cover over my shoulders to my chin and looked fully up at the ceiling.

My phone began to buzz, or was I tripping?

Buzz. Buzz. Buzz.

I looked over and saw my phone dancing.

My heart went from 0-100 real mf quick.

I pulled my blanket down off my body and looked at my hand.

It was trembling.

I took a deep breath and got up to look at my phone. I loved one eye and used the other to view the contact name.

"Tia," it read.

I accepted the call quickly.

"Thank god," I said as I pulled the phone to my ear.

<u>Chapter 13</u>

It was Friday. I hadn't gone to school since last week Friday, so I assumed today would be an okay day. If anything went wrong, the weekend would be there to save me.

I got dressed in an all maroon dress. I placed a bandana around my head and grabbed my white converse.

I looked at the time. I still had 14 minutes till I had to be at school.

I put on my shoes, grabbed my keys, and left the house.

As I drove down Gilmore street, the word "Starbucks" came to mind. I looked at the clock again.

12 minutes.

"What the hell!" I said as I made a left onto Jones.

Starbucks! Starbucks! Starbucks!

"Ah! Starbucks!" I shouted when my eye met the green and white logo.

I turned into the shopping center and saw that the Starbucks had a drive-through.

"This place is convenient…" I whispered to myself.

There were only two people in front of me when I arrived, and by the looks of it, they were teens like me.

I brought it to my home and opened up the app 'Snapchat'. I tapped on the name Nic and looked at his story.

He was wearing tan colored trousers and a red and black polo shirt. His hair was in the signature 'Nic' hairstyle, his shoes white, and a Rolex wristwatch, probably worth more than my whole life.

In his story he was smiling, it didn't look sincere, but it was believable. Harper on his right side latched on his arm and his arm wrapped around her shoulder.

Beep beep beep

"Oh shut," I looked in front of me and saw I was supposed to be ordering right now.

How much time did I spend on my phone? I drove up to the speaker thingy and placed an order for 2 cotton candy fraps.

"Scratch that, 3," I said to the man behind the voice in the machine.

One for me, one for Harper, and one for Tia. It was originally just for Tia and me, but if I didn't they for the ring leader, it would look shady.

Following the order, I drove up to the next window and paid the balance of $18.56. *When did drinks get so expensive?* They have me my drinks and I got back onto the road headed for school.

In three min three, I was pulling up into a parking space at school. I opened the door, for my drinks, backpack, and key.

Beep beep

My car sounded as I locked it. I began walking to the main entrance of the school, only to see my dearest new friend, Grant.

"Hey," he said slightly punching my back.

"What," I replied. *I was in a rush.*

"It was just a simple 'hey' Coy," he said.

"I know, I know, I'm sorry… I'm just in a bit of a rush."

I looked down at the time. I had only two minutes to deliver the drinks in my tray, put my things in my locker, and meet up with… I can't even remember who.

I hit myself on the head with my free hand and continued walking down.

Ding ding ding

I heard.

Oh my, the school bell. I was late for my first class, but who cares anyway, right?

I approached the turn that led to my locker. I put down the drinks on the floor near me before I turned. This was so that I'd be able to be fast and get out.

I walked swiftly down the hall and made a sharp left turn.

My eyes widened and I ran behind the corner I had just turned from.

I couldn't fathom what I'd just seen. I didn't want to believe what I'd just seen.

I peeked around the corner to verify if what I had seen had been real.

There it was.

Harper Faharo and Jonas Sanders in the hall, leaning on a few lockers, kissing like a newborn couple.

<u>Chapter 14</u>

"I thank the gods above for Saturday," Tia said as we walked around the grassy field at the butterfly lark.

"I clout agree with you more!" I said letting out a faint chuckle, but soon, a slight frown formed.

"What? Who do you see? What happened?" Tia said looking in all directions.

"Nothing." I tried adding a little smile, but it was useless. Tia could see right through me.

Thoughts had been crowding my head ever since yesterday in the hall.

Should I tell Tia?

Should I tell Nic?

All the questions filled my head leaving me unable to think, unable to focus.

I clenched Tia's hand, causing her to stop in her tracks and face me. I turned my body in her direction, standing still looking at her.

She could see the pain in my eyes, the guilt, the uncertainty.

"What happened?" She said.

My eyes became moist. I shut them tightly trying to
hold back my tears.

"I…"

"What is it Coy?"

"I saw, well… I caught Harper and Jonas together
in the hall."

Tia speed back, her eyes widened, and her Dora the
Explorer ice cream fell on the grass creating a large
orange, pink, and brown puddle.

<u>Chapter 15</u>

Tia had been walking back and forth in my room for the past 30 minutes from the looks of things, she was also confused.

We really only had two choices. Either snitch to Nic and get hated on by Harper and group, or ditch Nic, which, if they were ever to find out it would lead to hatred from Nic's party.

"How about we act like we don't know!" Tia blurted out.

"You? Act? Remember 3rd grade High School Musical play?" I said laughing.

"Yeah…" Tia said through clenched teeth.

Tia can't act, and even if she tried, she sounded like a monotones robot.

"So what are we going to do Tia?" I said frustrated.

"Let's change schools, our names, and get fake passports!" Tia said jokingly.

"You're not serious," I muttered.

"Obviously not, Coy," she replied.

Thirty minutes passed by and we had still not come up with a plan. I looked up at the ceiling and fell back on my bed letting out a long and depressing sigh.

Immediately, an idea came into my head. It wasn't terrible, but it wasn't great.

"Tia, I've got!" I blurted out loudly.

She turned to me, her eyes wide and a smile grew across her face.

Tia ran over to my bed like a 3-year-old toddler and sat down 'criss-cross applesauce.' Her attention on me and nowhere else.

I explained the plan to her and she clapped her hands louder than humanly possible.

"Let's do it!" She said letting out a faint smile.

We jumped off the bed, grabbed our bags from the corner, and headed out of the house.

I opened the garage, grabbed my key, and started my car. I backed out of the driveway quickly.

"Ready to put Plan X into gear?" I said to Tia, a smile crowding my face.

"Of course," she said, as we drove to the downtown supply shop.

Chapter 16

We had it all. The camera, the film, the untraceable phone, and a computer. We were getting everything together, over checking and making sure absolutely nothing went wrong. Otherwise, instead of rising in popularity, (that's not my goal lol) Tia and I would plummet lower than before.

"So explain to me exactly how we are going to do this?" Tia said hesitantly.

I looked up from my shaking, sweating hands, and took a deep breath.

"We are going to give Harper a box of chocolates and a teddy bear. We will do not next week Tuesday. It'll be her birthday, nothing suspicious. The teddy bear will have the cam in its eye. So when Harper has her locker open to hide her and," I made an ugly face, "Jonas smooching away, we will catch everything. It then goes directly to this computer here. The camera and the film are to take pictures, we'll be in hallway, snapping a few pics to throw in her locker and in the hallways." I finished out of breath.

Tia rapped ok her leg nervously, looking down at her thigh.

"What is it?" I said placing my hand over her own in an attempt to calm her down.

I could quickly tell it wasn't working.

"Why do you want to do this? Ruin her, Coy? I-," I cut her off.

"Tia, for God's sake, this is the same girl who sent you insulting texts in the 10th grade. The same girl who placed us below her because of clothing and shoes. The same fucking girl who sent a group of girls to beat you up on the bloody playground in the 5th grade!" I didn't notice I had began shouting until Tia removed her hand from where it laid under my own.

"I'm sorry," I said softly.

"It's okay. I understand. We got to do this. Not only for me, but for you, Coy." She brushed her fingers through her hair, bringing it back.

"Let's do this bitch," Tia said as an amazing large smile appeared on her face causing me to smile back.

Tia and I got off the couch in the television room in my house and went up to the loft. There was a lot of space there, enough to plan everything without distractions.

We got up to the loft and sat on the blanket next to the ash-colored drawers. I took out my jotter and began to think of what to write for the steps needed for everything to go correctly and according to plan.

Tia, you threw me a pen and I opened up my jotter
to the next blank page and began to write.

How To Succeed In Killing
A Pest

1. *Give items for birthday and make sure she
    places it in her locker.*
2. *Wait till nightfall to deactivate camera in
    bear*
3. *Use burner phone to send videos to Nic and
    the rest of the popular kids*
4. *Throw away the burner phone*
5. *Sit back and enjoy life*

It was wicked, but at least it was subtle and not
many people would see it.

"It's good," Tia said quietly to me.

"I know," I said, and we both laughed like wicked
witches of the west.

I slammed my jotter shut and stood up from the
soft, comfortable carpet.

"Wait for me!" Tia shouted as she ran up beside me.

"This is going to be good," I said smiling at Tia.

She turned her head and looked back at me with a
glimmering smile on her face.

67

"Agreed," She said as she proceeded down the
stairs and through the door of my room, slamming it
shut behind us.

<u>Chapter 17</u>

It was 6:27am. I had already take my bath and put on my makeup. I stood in front of my closet looking for an outfit to wear.

I flipped through and saw a plain white v-necked shirt. I took it off the hanger and threw it on my bed. As my eyes trailed the pants I had in my closet, I saw a light denim high waisted jeans that I had probably never worn. I pulled it out and walked over to my bed proceeding to put it on.

6:49 am the clock read this time. I hurried to my table and grabbed my phone. I went under the table, grabbed my white all-stars, and slipped my feet inside.

As I pushed open the door of my room, standing there was a cheater of the year, my father.

The blood drained from my face. I hadn't seen him since the divorce back in 2009.

I pushed past him, rolling my eyes. He trailed behind me like a lost puppy.

"Coy, we got to talk," he said sternly.

"No thanks, I have school, send me a text instead," I said like an annoyed mother.

"For God's sake, stop there! I am your father!" He shouted in anger.

I stopped in my tracks and turned around preparing myself for his abusive, psychopathic self.

"What do you want?" I said as I crossed my arms.

I had a goddamn plan to carry out and if I didn't leave in the next few minutes, I'd be late. And because it's Harper, she'll get carried away in the gifts and fake love.

"Coy, your credit card bill is getting ridiculously high. If you want to continue having one, slow down. And what were you even doing at the supply shop? Planning to murder a man?" He made a squeezed face.

"Something like that. Anyways, are you done?" I said putting out my hand and motioning my head.

He kept quiet and continued staring at me. Two minutes passed by and he was still standing in silence.

I turned my back and began walking down the stairs. When I was halfway down, my back arched inside, ankle twisted, and I tumbled down the stairs.

He pushed me.

My head hit the cold ground when I finally reach the bottom. I turned to look up at the top of the steps and saw the same brown-headed 6'2 white man standing. He was no longer angry or frustrated, rather happy.

I stood up and dusted off my clothes, making sure it was still white and intact. I grabbed my phone, which was now near the shoe rack instead of inside my pocket. A small dent had been formed on the back.

I took a long breathing session, trying to avoid shouting. After placing my phone in my back pocket, again, I grabbed my backpack and keys, opened the door, and flipped him the damn bird.

<u>Chapter 18</u>

I arrive at the school at exactly 6:53 am. My face is still red, but less noticeable than before.

I walked to my locker and opened it. I dropped my keys and bag inside, then grabbed the bear, chocolate, and my books.

"You ready?" I heard a girl say as I closed my locker.

Ugh, it was Tia (no offense, love ya).

"Yes!" I shouted happily.

"Me too," Tia replied.

We began walking to Harper's locker, trying to calm our nerves.

As we reach the corner, my heart almost fell into my ass. I took a deep breath and Tia and I continued walking.

Harper's locker was open, so she couldn't see us unless she closed it. The cameras were already in our pockets. They were roundish and flat, but they were still small enough to fit in our pockets.

Tia and I approached her locker, and right as we got there she walked out from behind her locker and shined the brightest, whitest, widest smile.

"Hey girls," Harper said cluelessly.

"Hey!" Tia and I both said smiling back.

I pulled out the bear and the Hershey chocolate from my backpack, nudging at Tia as well so she would stay calm.

"It's from Tia and me," I said boldly, still holding the demonic fake smile on my face.

As I handed her the bear, I tapped the eye twice in order to activate the footage taper.

"Oh my god!" Tears streamed from Harper's eyes that were once so cold to us.

"I'm so grateful! Thank you!" She said, pulling us into a tight hug.

Quickly, I pushed away, still maintaining my smile, and pulling Tia with me.

Harper still kept a smile, not knowing that we had pulled out. She looked down at the bear and chocolates one last time, before opening the cracked locker, and placing it inside perfectly.

My heart was beating her not to close my locker, and as she was about to, our part two appeared, Jonas.

"Bye Harper!" I said grabbing Tia and running around the corner.

I could honestly tell, that she hardly noticed.

As Tia and I peered around the corner, I saw the intimacy of them. It was never how I'd seen Harper and Nick. Maybe what we were doing would help her, rather than hurt her. Maybe she actually wanted to be with Jonas, not just for the sole purpose of hurting Nick.

As I continued staring, I observed two things about their 'not so secret' but 'secret' relationship.

Number one, Jonas paid an awful lot of attention to Harper. And trust me, when I'm saying that's hard, I mean, that's hard! The girl can blab.

And number two, he was affectionate towards her. When she was with Nick, the highest thing you would ever see them do was hold hands.

I turn to Tia, unable to think of what to say when the words just burst out of my mouth.

"Tia, I can't do it. I just can't, we are going to carry out the plan, but it is only going to Nic. No other person can ever know about it. This girl was terrible to us, but she's changing..." I paused, "And... we've gotta accept it." The sentence followed with a very long (and loud) gasp of air.

"Oh thank the lords!" Tia shouted happily.

"Shhh!" I said, pointing at Harper and Jonas in front of the open locker.

"So what are we gonna do with these cameras?" Tia asked in a questionable remark.

"Toss em," I said with a large smile on my face.

Tia began taking out her camera, ready to toss it to the side. My eyes widened and I shout whispered the word 'STOP' to Tia.

She immediately rearranged her position and put the camera in the bag beside her.

"Sorry," Tia said squeezing her face and shrugging her shoulders. I looked at her and rolled my eyes letting out a small giggle.

I turned around, deciding to get back to work before the bell rang. As I peered behind the wall, I saw what I needed all along. The footage, the bear had caught it all.

I faced towards Tia quickly raising my hands in celebration.

"We got it!" I said loudly hugging Tia.

"Shhh! It's all done." She replied as the bell rang for class.

Chapter 19

The school day was over and I was on my way to McDonald's to get a few things to eat.

I drove past Tropicana W and Sandy Road, making a left. There on the corner was the McDonald's

"Thank gods and goddesses," I said aloud.

Tia was on the passenger side of my car tapping away at her phone.

As I drove up to the drive-through at McDonald's I saw a familiar face.

Nic.

My stomach twisted at the thought of breaking his heart when he saw the video (I cared, but not truly). I quickly rolled up my window and drove up to the order machine.

"Hello, welcome to McDonald's, how may I help you today?" A man's voice beamed through the machine, sounding a little Southern.

"Yeah, please, could I get a 20 piece chicken nugget, large fries times two, and two double cheeseburgers?" I said politely.

"One second," he mumbled back as the items began appearing on the main black screen of the machine.

"What about me?" Tia whispered to me pouting like a god.

"You get the chicken nuggets and the large fries, I get the other fries and the burgers," I replied.

"Oh," She said, "fabulous!" She semi shouted, before looking back down at her phone.

What could be so interesting on that device? Golly! Oops, well at least now I know how my parents feel.

"Your total is $12.64 at the next window," he said loudly, "have a nice day."

I drove up to the next window with a $20 bill in my hand. The man standing in that small room with the microphone over his mouth opened the window.

"$12.67," he said a dull tone.

"Oh! Sorry!" I said as I handed him the $20 bill.

He pressed a few buttons on the screen in front of him. He gathered the change and printed my receipt.

"Have a great day," he said with an I hate my life smile.

"Thanks," I said back as I grabbed my change and receipt, driving up to the next window.

At the next window still a tall male, I couldn't tell who it was because he was standing backward.

He turned slowly, only to reveal his face.

"Here you go love," the boy said as he handed me my bag of food.

He closed the window and turned around only to turn back around and re-open the window.

"Tia? Coy?" He said.

"I literally wondered how long it would take you to realize who you were talking to Kingsley!"

Tia looked up from her phone and gulped air.

"Hey, Kingsley!" She said laughing.

"Hey, so girls, I have this mad story to tell you. I was in a plane right-!" He was cut off.

"KINGSLEY!" A big bulky man shouted.

"Gotta go!" Kingsley said as he closed the window and ran to attend to the big man who seems to be his manager.

Tia and I laughed and I drove off.

<u>Chapter 20</u>

Tia and I sat inside my room eating McDonald's and scrolling through social media.

"Where is the burner phone?" I said to Tia as I took a large bite of my burger and stuffed fries in as well.

"Here," Tia said as she threw it at me, dipping her nugget in BBQ and throwing it into her mouth

I took the phone from where it had landed and placed it by my side.

"Okay…" I inhaled and exhales dramatically getting a stare from Tia.

"Sorry," I said laughing.

I reached under my pillow and grabbed my MacBook Pro. I open the screen and type in my passcode.

I fiddled with the mouse and finally got the courage to click on 'live and recorded footage' in the corner of my home screen.

As I opened the program, the videos of Harper and Jonas started appearing. My chest at this point was pumping faster than ever

'100% download complete' the computer program pop-up said.

I clicked 'okay' under the message and we get reviewing the footage. I saved it to the library on my computer and cropped out the desired parts.

"Happy six months and happy birthday Harberry!" Jonas said hugging Harper and pecking her on the cheek.

"Thanks, baby, you too!" She said, " what did you get me?"

Jonas picked a small box from the side of his trousers and opened it up.

Oh my god...

"Oh my god!" Harper shouted in the footage, causing me to jump a little.

"Those are the Pandora 22K rose gold scented earrings I wanted!" She hugged Jonas tightly. "I love you," she said as she and Jonas kissed.

Perfect.

I cropped the footage and sent it to the burner phone, which took 5000 years to do.
I switched back to live footage and left my computer playing while I finished my food.

"What's in the eye of that bear Harper?" Jonas said. (Unfortunately, my dumbass didn't hear any of this).

"What do you mean?" Harper replied.

A hand covered the camera on the eye and plucked it out.

"A cam!" Jonas said as he looked directly into the small, almost invisible lense.

Jonas dropped it on the floor and smashed it. The footage ended there.

But for me, the Mcd's eating maniac was enjoying my food a little bit too much to notice.

Chapter 21

It was a new day. Everything felt brighter and more clear, but something, just something wasn't feeling right.

I pushed aside the thought and continued scrolling through social media. The previous night, I had sent the footage to Nic using the burner phone while Tia checked that everything in the plan, went according to plan. After everything was done, we disposed of all, and when I say all I mean ALL the items bought for the plan. Oh except for the cute Polaroid cameras.

After scrolling through Instagram for a while, I decided to get up. It was hump day after all. I put on a black dress that stopped right above my knees, put on my black converse, and tied my hair into a ponytail.

I ran downstairs and open the fridge, grabbing a large ice cream jar and a bowl to make cinnamon toast crunch.

I finished getting all my food, and preparing them, so I sat down at the main table and began eating.

Took one scoop of ice cream, followed with one scoop of cereal.

God this is good.

I unlock my phone and opened up the app Snapchat. I looked at a few friend's stories, but took interest in a few people, a.k.a. Nick and Harper.

My heart increased in speed, and it took all the courage I had in me, but I clicked Harper's story.

 The first picture I saw was halfway smiling with Saf, Grant, Jonas, Carol, Nadine, and Sam.

I tapped and saw the next post which read, "friends, friends, inspections begin today." I tapped again, "who can I even trust?" I tapped a third time and a picture of Harper smiling but it looked like she had been crying, "free. at. last." it read.

I clicked out of Harper story and proceeded to Nic's story.

His first post was an effortless, and shirtless, mirror picture, featuring his hand in his hair.

I admired the picture for 10 minutes (not literally) then clicked to another post. My heart fluttered and my face filled with joy. It read, "Free to go for her, the one I truly want."

I clicked off button on my phone and fell back in my seat.

"Oh my God," I said as milk squirted out and near my bowl.

I picked up my phone again, but this time to make a call. I went to my contacts and dialed the number.

"Hey," the person on the line said.

"How are you," I said back.

"I'm okay what do you want, Coy?" she replied.

"Harper I wanna know what you meant by when you said you are…"

"Nic and I broke up and with Jonas. I think Saf set me up or Grant, but you and Tia are off of my suspects list. Just pretend none of this ever happened." Harper cut the phone.

My heart was pounding fast, but I wanted to stay calm and enjoy my day.

How did Harper know someone set her up?

I ran to my computer in my room and opened up the security camera program.

Oh. No.

The deactivate button was still red, indicating we had never turned it off.

The live footage was just showing the floor, and in the corner I could see a bear leg. The camera was just showing the floor, and in the corner I could see a very long leg. The footage looked cracked and dirty, probably indicating someone had taking it out from the bear and stepped on it.

I quickly pressed deactivate and slammed my computer screen shut.

" I'm done for. I'm so done. for dad I'm obviously done." I said as I waddled down the steps.

I went back to the table and turned on the television, switching to Disney channel. That's so Raven was playing. At least something could provide peace in my life.

As I continued eating my food and watching TV, my phone began to ring.

I peered at the screen and saw the name Tia. I let it finish ringing, then I put my phone on 'do not disturb' mode.

I finished my food and went to the couch to get a closer view of the television. As I watched I dozed off and fell asleep.

<u>Chapter 22</u>

It was Saturday, meaning I survived the week without Harper's wrath. The whole week, well what was left of it, I had been avoiding people. I didn't want to seem suspicious, but with Nic on the loose, and Harper on a killing machine, it's better I stayed clear of them.

I sat in my car, driving to a nearby fast food place called In-N-Out. Their food was like heaven. So, when I wasn't in the mood for my regular McDonald's, I would go there.

I parked in front of the building and climbed down from my jeep, shut the door of my jeep, and made sure the doors are locked.

Walking into the In-N-Out, I was enlightened by the smell of fries and burgers. Food, the only thing that could make a girl happy.

"Hello, what can I get for you?" A man at the cashier named 'Lan' said.

"Um, just a cheeseburger and fries, my usual," I said with a faint smile.

"Your total is $7.98!" He said as I gave him a $10 bill.

He handed me my change and in less than two minutes my food was presented to me.

"Have a great day!" he said with a smile.

"You too, Lan!" I hollered back.

I carried my tray and went to sit down at the nearby empty, but clean, table. I sat down quickly and picked up my burger with a few fries and began to stuff bites into my mouth like a maniac.

A voice beamed from the front of my table.

"Oh hey mind if I join?" the voice uttered.

I picked up a napkin and wiped my mouth before looking up. Oh, and who else could it be? Nic fucking Reed. I closed my eyes and rolled them then I looked directly at him with a non-teeth smile (not trying to ruin my image anything with the piece of meat in my teeth).

"Sure," I murmured unenthusiastically.

Nic pulled out a chair, I guess he been sitting out before coming over to my table and sitting down beside me.

"So how are you, Coy?" Nic said weakly rubbing his hand on the back of his neck.

It must be a signature move for him, his hand is always somewhere on his head.

"Could be better, uh, you?" I said through a half stuffed chewing mouth.

 "Really great!" he said smiling for no reason.

I looked down at my burger and fries, back up at Nic, then back at my food. As I reached for my burger Nick uttered another sentence.

"So, uh, Coy, you know that school dance on Friday night right?" he asked shyly.

"Yeah," I said eating a few fries.

I was so oblivious I couldn't tell he was trying to ask me out. I might have seemed rude or disrespectful on my behalf, but I was fed up mentally and physically.

I looked down at the floor and reached for my phone, I pressed the home button, then began typing in my code.

"Look, Nic, if you're trying to say something—,"

Nick grabbed my chin and smashed into mine. *I was in heaven.*

Resisting from temptation and coming to my senses, (which was awful because it would or will lead to the ending of a perfect kiss) I pulled back opening my eyes wide.

"Will you go to the dance with me Coy Clent?" Nic said as he gasped for air silently.

"Sure," I said casually as I picked up my things and my tray, threw it away, turned around, and exited the fast food place.

I unlocked my car door, and opened it up, jumped inside with the biggest smile on my face, and drove off.

"You make me feel like a dangerous woman, something 'bout, something 'bout you, makes me blah blah blah blah blah blah blah blah!" I sang as I danced around the closet in my room.

"We get it Coy, you love Africana Grande's song. Now stop before you burst my eardrums!" Kingsley shouted from the corner of my room.

"It's my choice!" I shouted back and continued, but this time humming.

I flipped through my hangers with clothing and brought out a black cropped top with a hugging skirt, that ended right above my knees.

I hopped like a bunny as I put each leg into my skirt. Following that tragedy, I slipped into my top and began walking to my bed.

"Kingsley!" I shouted like an angry grandma.

"Yes, mother!" he replied back, as he walked towards me and sat down.

"I gots to tell you something…" I said in a low tone and peered over at the door.

My mom was home, and she is a mother tracking bot. As in nothing goes unknown in this house. It used to be a lot worse, but after the death of my brother, Asher, and the divorce going on between my mom and my father at the time, she was forced to calm down and live a calmer life.

"Oh, okay, I understand…" Kingsley said smiling as he closed my room door before coming to sit back down near me.

"Spill it girl," Kingsley said leaning in as if I were going to whisper in his ear.

"Well, I was at In-N-Out," I said in a low tone.

"Bomb as fuck," Kingsley said back.

"Yeah, I know. Well anyways, I was eating and then Nic came up to me saying he had a question to ask me. Then he kissed me and asked to go to the lover's dance on Friday." I said gasping for air.

"But no big deal!" I said smiling.

Kingsley's mouth dropped open and he let out a big gasp/

"Oh my god," Kingsley said as he stood up from the bed and began walking around the room causing me to be dizzy.

"Could you stop that please," I said politely as I looked at Kingsley.

"Yeah, sorry." He said as he came back to the bed and sat down.

"I thought he and Harper were still doing that odd thing they considered a relationship," Kingsley said through furrowed brows.

"Oh yeah, you've been a little out of the loop, Tia and I sabotaged Harper because she was cheating on Nic, so he left her and now Harper is dating Jonas publically." I said out of breath yet again.

"Where have I been?" Kingsley shouted as he fell back on my bed with his hand over his eyes.

"Working at McDonald's…" I muttered.

"Yeah, you're probably right," He replied back as he sat back up with his hands by his side.

"I'm asking dumb questions, what did you say to his question? Did you act like a badass or a shy baby? Did you kiss him back? Oh, and uh nice job with what you and Tia did, I probably would have fucked up." Kingsley said like a celebrity who was freestyling on the spot.

"I said a simple, sure, I looked like a motherfucking badass too. And well um, I kissed him back, but just a bit, and thanks, I know!" I stated as I flipped my hair after making that statement.

"Aye, that's my girl!" Kingsley said as he patted my head as if I were a dog.

"Thanks," I removed his hand from where it lay on the top of my head, "anyways, what are we going to do today? I don't want Sunday to go to waste."

"Oh…" Kingsley clenched his teeth, "we all already had it planned out, I just can't tell you till we are far enough and can't turn back."

"What? Who is we? And what did you guys plan?" I stood up from my bed and Kingsley followed.

"Here is a swimsuit and some cute flip flops, go outside and get in the car," Kingsley said handing me a bag that seemed to come out of nowhere.

He pushed me and told me to run down the stairs. He grabbed an empty backpack from my room and placed my things inside, as well as hi sown. Kingsley came down the stairs and tapped me on my back.

"Open the door!" He shouted as he motioned a 'go away' sign.

I opened the door, and right outside was a large 7 seater jeep. Black paint and black wheels as well.

And inside the car were hollering teenagers that went by the names Saf, Harper, Jonas, Nic, Cleo, Tia, and Grant, golding water and pool items. They all looked colorful and basically clothless.

"Get in the car bitch!" Saf shouted as she honked the horn.

Kingsley gave me a shove from the back and closed my house door after shouting, "Bye Ms. Clent!"

"Oh boy, this is going to be a long day," I said as Cleo, Tia, and Kingsley dragged me into the car.

As I hopped inside and they shut all the doors a voice from inside shouted, "Vegas Baby!" Right as I placed my hand on the door so I could escape, they drove off in a flash.

Chapter 24

All I could see was cacti, tumbleweeds, and more and more dust.

A while ago we had past Ghost Town. So we were actually close to Vegas. I knew the saying, "All that happens in Vegas stays in Vegas." I honestly don't know what I am going to tell my mom, but it better be believable.

I looked outside the window of the car and leaned up against it. I went into the bag Kingsley had packed and pulled out my phone. I scanned my fingerprint and automatically went to messages.

I tapped the group chat named 'Queens' that featured Kingsley, Tia, and me. I then began typing in the chat.

"You guys are beyond dead when we get back, how could you just leave me out of the loop. You all planned this, and I took no part. Am I a visitor or a guest now?" I pressed send and the blue bubble appeared.

I stared at my screen, then a grey typing bubble appeared on the screen. 5 seconds later, a text came in from Tia.

"None of us planned it, it was Harper, Jonas, and Nic. They decided it would be a great idea, so we could all go back to being that tight clique we were before. And plus, it is senior year!" Tia typed.

"Yeah! So let's have fun buzz," Kingsley sent right after Tia.

I shut off my phone and dozed off in hopes of waking up when we reached Vegas.

<u>Chapter 25</u>

"Coy, wake the fuck up if you want food!" Grant said as he tapped my cheeks (the facial kind).

My eyes instantly widened at the word 'food.' I instantly sat up straight and cleaned my face off with my hands.

I looked around and saw that we were at McDonald's.

Salvation has come.

Nic was driving the car, so he pulled up to the side of the order machine and began to speak.

"Hello, welcome to the finest establishment here in Vegas, Mcdonald's." The lady voice that was coming from inside the machine beamed.

Nic did a fake, but bearable, laugh then began to talk.

"Yes, um, there are quite a few of us, so the order might take a while. And when I say another person's name before a food item, please make sure to separate them into different bags."

"K," the Hispanic sounding lady replied.

I love McDonald's but I never said the workers were kind. If kindness is what you're searching for, head over to Chick-fil-a.

"For I, a Big Mac, large fry, and a sprite," Nic said, as the items appeared on the black screen.

"Harper, a large chicken salad, apple pie, and diet coke." He paused and asked Grant, Cleo, Kingsley, Tia, and I for our orders.

"Grant, Double quarter pounder meal, Cleo will have the same too. Kingsley, a chicken nugget 20 piece and large fries with a cone, Tia will also have the same, Jon-ass will have a Big Mac meal with a large Dr. Pepper, Saf will have the same thing too. As for the beautiful Coy, she will have a chicken nugget 10 piece, 2 double cheeseburgers, and a large fry with a Fruitopia," Nic said as everyone in the car peered over at him then at me.

They all began to laugh, but seized when the machine lady began to speak again.

"Your total is $63.92," she said in a bland tone.

"Thanks," Nic said as he drove up to the next window.

He gave the woman who had been talking to us an $100 bill, or a Benjamin as the kids these days call it, and she gave him his change.

Nic drove up to the next window and began handing each of us our bags of food one by one. As he drove

off from the drive-through, everyone said their
thank yous to Nic.

"So what hotel are we staying at by the way?" I said
chewing my chicken nuggets,

"Oh, nothing big, just Wynn." Nic said as he
adjusted his mirror and smiled back at me.

I choked on my food and began tapping my chest.

"Wynn? As in like $20,000 a night Wynn? Mall
Cops 2 Wynn? Fucking beautiful as fuck Wynn?" I
said as my face went red.

"Yes Coy, do you wanna choke again? Or are you
going to wash it all down with your drink?" Cleo
said sarcastically.

"Oh yeah, thanks…" I muttered as I drank my
fruitopia quarter way down.

As Nic drove along the strip of Vegas, my eyes
were mesmerized. Vegas had a fresh look unlike
Cali where some places looked new, and others,
really old and dirty.

We approached a brown and gold building labeled
"Wynn" at the top. Next to it, a twin building called
"Encore."

"Wow," came out of almost all the people in the
cars mouths.

"I know," Nic said in a mocking tone.

As we got closer to the entrance of the hotel, beautiful palm trees and people filled the streets. There were many lights now, so I couldn't imagine what it would look like at night.

We were approaching the valet for cars. Once we reached the front, we all got out of the car, and took our bags. A man named Valentine took us to the golden doors at the front of the building.

He pushed it open and everyone's mouths hung open.

"Welcome to the Wynn Hotel!" The man said, "Enjoy your stay!"

We all walked inside looking side to side. I notice that my clique was a little underdressed in jeans and swimsuits. I just thank the gods that I wore something semi-decent.

I walked around with Sad and Tia, admiring the lobby, which in my opinion was larger than my whole house.

"Guys, girls! Come on, we gotta check-in before they give our rooms to other people!" Nic shouted from the enormous lobby.

As we all came to Nic, I noticed the decorations. Everything was put together so nicely, even the workers.

Some workers wore a dark red and white outfit, while other workers wore a brown and white uniform. They all also had a golden name tag though.

We got to the check-in counter and were greeted by a very beautiful African woman named Pamela. She looked like someone in her early to mid-thirties. Her hair was curly and beautifully done, her makeup was simple, yet elegant, and she had a thick accent, not very sure where from though.

"Hello, my name is Pamela and I am one of the head managers here at Wynn. May I please have your name?" She said smiling at Nic who was in front of us all.

"Nicholas Reed," he said as she began typing something into the computer.

"Okay, here I see Nicholas Reed and a party of eight. You will be staying in rooms 204, 206, 208, and 210." Pamela said as she handed us the door keys.

"The first room is reserved for, hold on, let me check here, yes, Harper Faharo and Jonas Sanders. In the second we have Kingsley Seyl and Saf Grey, and in the third, Grant Simon and Cleo Robinson.

Last but not least, Nicholas Reed and Coy Clent are in the last room." Pamela finished and looked back up at Nic and the rest of us.

"Yes, that is correct," he said as he turned around and winked in my direction.

Oh boy.

"In the morning we have a complimentary breakfast, as well as lunch during the afternoon, and dinner in the night. We provide room service and much more. If you need anything, please don't hesitate to call the front desk, we are always around." Pamela said and then motioned a man to take our bags.

The man carried out bags into a golden car thing and we went up to our rooms on the nearest elevator.

When we got to the floor, everybody entered their designated rooms. I entered mine (and Nic's) room. He followed behind me and then closed the door.

I turned on the light and immediately had an excitement attack.

THE ROOM WAS LITERALLY LARGER THAN MY WHOLE HOUSE, MAKING THE LOBBY BIGGER THAN MY WHOLE NEIGHBOURHOOD.

"Oh my god," I said as I dropped my side bag onto the floor then jumped onto one of the beds and laid back.

"I can finally stretch my legs?" I shouted as I reached for the remote and Switched to 'E!'

Keeping Up With The Kardashians was playing so that meant I would be up for a long time.

"Coy, a stack of money is here in case you need to purchase anything," Nic said as he pointed to the counter near my bed.

"Thanks," I said as I kept my eyes glued to the screen.

Nicholas chuckled and walked towards the second bed in a completely different part of the hotel room.

"Goodnight, Coy," He said as he turned off his lamp and began to doze off.

<u>Chapter 26</u>

I woke up in a foggy mess. Nic had probably 'unknowingly' taken his shower with the door open.

I sat up and slapped the top of my head. I opened my eyes wider and peered around the room.

"Good morning," Nic said as he approached the bed. His hair wet and only a small towel around his waist.

I covered my eyes quickly and fell back onto the bed where I had lied before. *Is this torturing me or seducing me?*

"Oh come on, stop that, we are no longer kids, Coy. And you've probably seen maybe a little more than this on social media!" Nic said laughing.

I sat up and fixed my eyes on his face trying not to look down. Nic walked over to the foot of the bed and leaned over to get the remote. As he tried to stand up straight, his towel fell down.

"Oh my god!" I said as a gasp came out from my mouth.

Nic smiled very wide and looked down, then back up at me.

"What? You've never seen a good view?" He said teasingly.

Nic walked over to the windows with curtains and drew them wide open exposing himself to not only me but the rest of Vegas.

"Put on your fucking towel, Nic!" I said frustrated.

"I'd rather just get dressed babe." He replied as he walked to the closet, grabbing his underwear and began putting it on.

"A bit more PG for you, love?" Nic said as he grabbed an outfit and began putting it on.

"Honestly, what do you want from me?" I said when he finally finished putting on his clothes.

Nic looked over at me from the side of the room where he was and began coming towards me.

"Coy Clent, please go out on a date with me," Nic said as he grabbed my hand and kissed it.

My cheeks were red and all the air in my body was coming out. I looked at Nic straight in the eyes and took a very deep breath.

"Yes, I guess." I said as I got up and hugged him.

He held me tight and brushed my hair behind my ear, only to kiss my cheek and whisper a cute sentence into my ear.

"I'll pick you up on Wednesday night when we get home, beautiful."

106

<u>Chapter 27</u>

It was Tuesday morning and today would be our last day in Vegas. Yesterday, after that whole Nic drama show, all we did was walk along the strip and buy a bunch of merchandise.

I kind of went overboard and spent $200 on my credit card. But, I mean, it IS Vegas, so go big or go home.

Today we were just going to see the blue man group show and hit the pool then leave Vegas around 3 pm.

Over the last few days, Nic and I definitely got to know each other more and got a bit closer --- even if it was a little inappropriate.

I peered over at the clock and saw the time. It read 8:49. I was dressed and so was Nic.

The show was to begin at 9, so we had to start going otherwise we would be absolutely late for such an amazing performance.

As I opened my mouth to call Nic, he walked into the room with Adidas joggers and a black top.

"Ready to go?" Nic said as he brushed his hair with his fingers.

"Yeah," I said and smiled.

Nicholas put out his hand indicating that I should hold it, and as I did.

We walked out the door and met up with the rest of the gang in the lobby.

When Tia got a glimpse of me and Nicholas holding hands, she gave me a thumbs up but made sure nobody else saw.

Harper and Jonas were smiling and in each others arms when we arrived, and it stayed that way till we got to MGM where the show was taking place.

When we got inside the theatre, we all sat down next to who we wanted to, then the show began.

<u>Chapter 28</u>

It was 2:37 pm. All of us were worn out from swimming but somehow managed to take out baths.

Nic was resting in his part of the room and I was watching --- well channel surfing with Tia.

"Oh, yeah!" Tia whispered and then let out a small laugh.

"When did you and Nic start dating? And why didn't you tell me? I thought we were best friends?" Tia said looking straight at me.

"We are not best friends Tia, we are practically sisters. I am not dating Nic, and if I was, I would obviously tell you." I said as I grabbed her hand and squeezed it before letting go.

The door opened in the corner of the room and out came Nic. He had changed his clothes to a white top and jogger shorts.

He wiped his eyes a few times and let out a yawn. He turned to the fridge area and brought out a coke from the night before.

"You guys ready to go?" Nic said as he shut the fridge and took a sip of his coke.

"Yeah," Tia and I both replied as we stood up from the bed.

Nic grabbed the keys and the bad he had brought along with him then opened the door.

"Goodbye beautiful hotel, and I hope to visit you soon," I whispered looking around at my surroundings.

Nic, Tia, and I walked out the front and began walking to the lobby.

The other members of the clique were already there as usual.

Nic went to the front desk to where Pamela was.

"Thank you, ma'am," he said as he gave her the room keys and a hundred dollar note.

"Thank you, love! We hope to see you again soon." Pamela said as she smiled as she put away the money and keys.

Nic walked to the front door of the hotel, indicating we were going, and we all followed from behind.

Chapter 29

Tonight was the big night. My first official date with Nic. Hopefully no inappropriate moves or seductive actions.

I went into my closet and looked for the most boujee dress I could find.

Red was too formal, white was too clean, gold was too blinding, but black was just right.

The only two black dressed in my closet were beautiful but never worn. I picked up both of them by the hanger and inspected them.

The first had a halter sleeve style and hugged my body all the way down then came out a little at the end. The second one had off the shoulder arms and also hugged my body but stopped at just right under my knees.

"Second it is," I said as I put the first dress and the vacant hanger back into my closet.

I'm honestly not a high heel girl, but if would be terrible if I wore sneakers on a date.

I looked at my shoe rack to see if there were any nice and classy shoes I could wear. My eye spotted a pair of black flats that were very glossy.

I changed my clothes very fast the dropped the older ones onto my bed.

I heard my mom shouting something from downstairs but it was quite hard to hear.

"What?" I shouted back loudly.

"Someone is at the door!" she shouted back much louder than the first time.

I put on my earrings and grabbed my small black side bag with my phone inside.

I left the door of my room and headed to the stairs.

"Oh shit, my necklace!" I said quietly as I felt my neck and ran back to my room grabbing and placing my necklace on.

As I ran down the stairs I could hear the knocking.

"I got the door, mom," I said as I laughed.

I opened the door, and there standing was Nic in a black suit and tie.

"Wow," we both said at the same time feeling astonished.

"Um, here…" Nic said as he brought out a rose from his back.

"Thanks," I said as I grabbed it and smiled.

"Shall we?" Nic replied and held out his arm for me.

"Finally," I said and we both laughed.

I grabbed his hand and stepped out of the doorway grinning like a ninny.

"Bye Mom, love you!" I shouted and shut the front door.

<u>Chapter 30</u>
We walked into the door of the restaurant and it was
named 'Belle.' The setting was dark and set with
candles in various areas. The air smelled of
delicious food and lavender. It was absolutely
stunning. Haha, but imagine how much this would
cost.

I frowned at the thought, but quickly brushed it off
to avoid ruining this date.

Nic and I walked to the front counter and were
quickly escorted to our table.

"Here is your menu sir, ma'am, have a goodnight,"
the butler said and began to walk off.

Nic and I sat down and began to look at the menu.

"Uh, what are you going to get?" I said shyly to
Nic.

"Not really sure, maybe the parmesan cheese
spaghetti with meatballs and some coca-cola," he
paused and looked back down at his menu, "or we
could both get burgers and fries like regular
teenagers."

We both began laughing, but it quickly died off
when the waiter came to the side of the table.

"Are you ready to order?" The waiter said releasing
a strong but soft British accent.

"Um, yes. We will have burgers and fried, two plates, with a coke," I interrupted.

"And a fruitopia!" I said to the waiter.

"Will that be it?" The waiter said.

"Yes, thank you," Nic said and the waiter began to walk away.

Nic and I both giggle a little under our breaths.

"So, when do you think the food will be ready," I muttered.

"It usually takes just a few-," The waiter came to the table holding our food.

"Here you go, if you need anything else, just press the bell under that cover," he pointed at a cover in the center of our table, put the food in front of each of us, then walked off like usual into the darkroom.

"Ready to try it?" Nic said to me as he picked up his burger with some fries.

"Absolutely," I picked up my burger and a few fried as well and we both took large bites.

"Holy god, this is the shit," I said as I stuffed more food into my face.

Nic laughed, nodded his head, and did the exact same thing.

After sitting in silence for 10 minutes, enjoying our burgers and perfectly seasoned fries, Nic and I dusted off our hands and began looking back at each other.

To remove the tension between us, I picked up my drink and began sipping slowly.

"Coy, you know the dance on Friday, right?" I continued sipping my drink, "Do you still want to go?" I nodded my head but refused to remove my lips from my drink, "Coy, it's not just any regular dance, it's prom." I choked on my drink. I literally thought it was just another lovers dance.

I put my cup down and began looking at Nic.

"What do you mean? Prom? It's prom?" I said in a low tone.

"Yeah, that's why I asked you, Coy. I wanted it to mean something to me." My cheeks flushed red.

"So, I have to buy, like, a dress? An expensive dress? And heels?" I said sounding like a child.

"Not necessarily. What you have on right now is absolutely stunning." Nic looked down at his drink and picked it up.

God, he had a way with words. It just turned my insides upside down.

He quickly finished his drink and I followed by his lead.

"Hey, Coy?" Nic said looking awfully nervous than before.

"Yeah?" I replied back.

"Would you like to be my girlfriend?"

My jaw immediately fell open. I quickly turned my head to the side and my screeching face before turning back.

"I'm. I. I'd honestly love to, but…"

"No, Coy, please."

I inhaled deeply and let it back out.

"Okay, Nic, I will. I'd love to." I said and smiled widely.

<u>Chapter 31</u>

I've only been to school once this week, and if I keep this up, my attendance will be terribly alarming.

I heard a knock on my door and began walking down to the door.

"Who is it?" I shouted at the closed door.

No reply.

I opened the door and found a package on the doorstep.

What the fuck?

I picked it up and went into the house. I walked into the kitchen and grabbed a knife on the table and quickly cut open the package.

Inside was a golden gift box with a bow. I pulled off the bow and quickly uncovered the box to see a beautiful golden dress.

It was long and hugged my body, then at the bottom it came out in the style of a mermaid dress. It was also strapless.

I picked up the dress and after doing so, it revealed gorgeous Louis V heels.

Under one of the heels, a cute note was left. I opened it up and almost began to cry.

Dear Coy,
*   Words cannot describe how I feel about you. I know you had a little trouble with the idea of prom yesterday, so I bought you a little something JUST INCASE you wanted something new.*
*   Yours Truly,*
*   Nic*

I put everything on the table perfectly and posted it on Snapchat. Immediately, Tia and Harper replied… Tia's message said, "Oh my god, you're dating!" I simply replied with a thumbs up and smiling face, indicating it was true.

My heart began pounding faster as I looked at the notification telling me Harper had messaged me. I used all the courage in my body and clicked on the message. "Oh wow, congrats, love you."

"What the fuck?" I said a little too loud.

I mean, it's better than a catfight. Oh well.

I carried all my things and went to my room.

I decided to do my classes online rather than at school today. It was honestly way better than going physically. And this way, I'd have time to search for makeup artists.

After finishing up my assignments online, I called up a makeup artist I found on a youtube channel. We agreed on a time and cut the phone.

I was honestly so ready for tomorrow, and nothing could ruin my day; absolutely nothing.

<u>Chapter 32</u>

It was 7:15 pm and Nic would be here at 7:30.

My makeup was already done and I had my clothing on. I carried my shoes that Nic had bought me and went to the sitting room downstairs.

My mother was in the kitchen with her large camera, ready to take pictures.

Ding dong, ding dong.

"Oh Christ, here we go," I said under my breath.

"I got the door!" MY mom shouted loudly before running to the door with a camera dangling from her neck.

She opened the door and gasped immediately.

"Wow, aren't you handsome! I'm Ms. Clent, nice to meet you. Thank you for taking out my daughter, she can be a little lonely, but I'm sure with you she'll be okay, but take care of her, alright? Oh yeah, thank you for the items you bought her!" My mom finally finished and took a deep breath.

"Pictures! Pictures! Oh, my baby is growing up so fast!" My mom motioned us to the stairs and turned on her camera.

We rook multiple pictures, some of Nic putting on that cheesy flower thing around my wrist, us hugging, and even some pictures of us laughing.

Nic and I got up from our pose and walked to the front door. My mom opened it and showed us the path out the door.

"Bye, love you!" Shouted.

Nic and I got into the car and drove off.

<u>Chapter 33</u>

The room was beautiful. I didn't know the gym could ever look so nice. Lights were everywhere, music was playing, and the room was full of food.

As Nic and I walked hand in hand, the attention began to drift towards us. I noticed Tia in the corner of the room, she was asked out by a boy named Lambert. He was hot and rich, but not my type.

I peered around the room but was unable to see Harper.

Harper? Miss prom? Impossible.

"I'm glad you came with me Coy!" Nic hollered over the music.

"Yeah, me too!" I shouted back and smiled.

"Would you like anything to drink?" He said like a gentleman.

"Yeah, just punch, thanks!" I said as I kissed him on the cheek.

He smiled and ran off to get the punch on the other side of the gym.

I put my purse on the chair I was sitting on to preserve our seats, then I went to the lady's room.

I pushed open the door to find an empty bathroom.
"Thank god," I said to myself.

I went into a stall and did my business before
flushing and exiting the stall.

I washed my hands before hearing another flush in
the bathroom.

What the fuck?

Out came Harper. She walked up to the mirror
farthest away from me and began reapplying
makeup.

"Hey, Harp!" I said smiling.

She looked at me a fake smile before turning back
to the mirror rolling her eyes.

"I love your dress, did you get it at the thrift shop?"
Harper said and began laughing.

I began laughing along too, hoping it was a joke.

"Where is Nic anyways?" She said as she smacked
the lip gloss she had just put on.

"He is outside, in the gym." I dried my hands with a
napkin, "where is Jonas?"

"Why would it matter to you Coin? You don't support me." She pouted her bottom lip and then began to laugh again.

"Harp, what do you mean? I truly-,"

"Don't," Harper said and shoved me a little bit.

"Oh my, Harper…" I looked at my wrists and they started bleeding. My old cuts started reopening.

"Oh my god, you're also a suicidal bitch, no way!" Harper laughed and inspected my arms.

I turned on the sink and began to wash away the blood that had spilled out onto my wrists.

"Harper, that was before. What is going on with you? What did I do?" I got a napkin and dabbed the areas that were still bleeding.

Harper walked around me in a circle and inspected me head to toe. She suddenly stopped right in front of me and smiled really wide. She took another step closer to me and grabbed my wrists with a harsh force.

"Oh fuck, Harper, stop!" I whisper shouted to avoid the attention of others outside.

Harper squeezed tighter causing the blood to come out once again, and this time a lot more.

My eyes began to water and tears streamed down my cheeks.

"Harper, stop…" I whispered in a silent weep.

"I know what you did Coy. I may seem stupid, but after this, you will surely know my true colors. Just prepare for your life to get a whole lot worse." Harper threw down my wrists and spat on the floor in front of me before leaving the bathroom.

I looked down at my wrists and began to try harder.

"What have I done?" I looked into the mirror at my reflection, "What the fuck did I do?" I shouted in a medium tone.

I turned on the sink and washed my wrists once again. I dried my hands, fixed up my face, put on a fake happy face, and returned to my table where Nic was not sitting down.

"Was it Harper?" Nic said as he gave me a weak smile.

My heart dropped.

"No, why?" I replied maintaining a neutral face.

"I saw her come out of the bathroom, but I mean, oh okay, if you're sure." Nic smiled wide and pointed at the seat I had been sitting in.

"Oh, yeah!" I sat down and looked at Nic directly in
the eyes.

"So… Why do you like me?" I questioned and took
another sip from my punch.

"You're just. Different."

"Different, how?" I said as I furrowed my brows.

"Special, unique, crazy, outgoing, just everything a
guy hadn't noticed. And I was one of them. When I
got the chance to know you more, I took it. You are
special, Coy Clent," Nic paused and looked around
the gym before looking back at me, "and that's why
I love you."

*What the fuck. Oh shit, I am doomed. Love? Is he
that crazy? Looks must be deceiving. Imagine what
he will think of me when Harper tells everyone IF
Harper tells anyone.*

"Oh, sorry, I shouldn't have, Coy," Nic grabbed my
hand and was looking straight at me, "I'm sorry, I
shouldn't have of said it."

"It's okay Nic. There is nothing wrong… I'm just at
a loss of words. That's because I… I love you too."
I said and a tear rolled down my cheek.

Nic stood up from his seat and came over to the side
of the table where I was sitting.

"Hey," Nic said causing me to turn my head in his direction, "Why are you crying?"

Nic used his hand and wiped the tears off my face before bending down to my level.

"I'm not going to hurt you, Coy, because I truly do love you," Nic smashed his lips into mine, and this time there was no backing out.

We were together, no more distractions. At this point in time, no one can break our bond.

Chapter 34

Six great months. No sign of Harper and her threat of exposing me. No bad publicity or body shaming issues. Just six good- great months together with Nicholas Reed. Maybe dreams do come true.

I had five minutes until I had to go to school and I was actually excited, we only had two months until senior year would end. Plus, Harper and I are friends again and she gave Nic and I tickets for a show next week

Today Harper messaged me. She had a surprise waiting at school for me. I was really curious because over the past few months she has sent me so many gifts, and over the past few months, she has seemed to regret everything she did on prom night.

I picked up all the things I needed for school then went to the garage.

"I like to chacha, aye, with the Dominicans," I hummed as I got into the car and drove off.

When I got to the school parking lot and got out of the car, all eyes were on me. People looked in disgust, others in joy, while others whispered and laughed.

What could be wrong? Is it my outfit? No, it's okay… No tears or exposed parts. Is it my hair? No.

it's just curled. My face? No! It's just fine... Then what is it?

As I continued walking through the whole parking lot, the audience grew.

"Dumbass bitch," I heard as I entered the doors of the school.

There I saw Harper plastering a bunch of posters all over the wall.

BACKSTABBER ALERT
Coy Clent
Ruined Harper's life for fun and entertainment, stole her boyfriend, lies to everyone, cuts herself (just look at her wrists), and cries herself to sleep.

My eyes began to swell as I read the painful words.

"Good morning students, it is Saf Grey and Tia Fields, and welcome to the announcements!" The speaker in the halls boomed and busted with sound.

Harper put her hand around my shoulder and kept a wide and malicious smile on her face.

"Today we are going to be covering the story of the Exposing of Coleen Clent, otherwise known as Coy," Tia said on the speakers enthusiastically.

"So, let's get the tapes rolling," Sad said and pressed play on a phone, I guess.
The audio started to play and I could recognize the voices. It was me. Not only me, nut Tia, but she had also been playing me.

"So what are we going to do Tia?" It was me, it was actually me... The tapes continued.

"Let's change schools, our names, and get fake passports."

"You're not serious."

"Obviously not," Tia said back.

The audio was cut here because of a loud thinking period we had, or at least I had.

"Tia, I've got it!"

I sounded so foolish.

I took a few minutes to explain the whole plan to Tia.

"Let's do it," Tia said uncomfortably.

"Ready to put Plan X in gear?"

I sounded like a gotdamn mastermind.

"Of course," Tia said and then I heard her pick up the phone in the audio.

"1st part complete," Tia whispered into the microphone then cut off the audio.

"Well, there you go Light View High, the reign of Coin Clent stop- ends here and now," Saf said over the speaker.

"Have a good day!" Tia said after and the announcement was over.

Boos, paper, insults, and objects were coming at me from left and from the right.

Harper whispered into my ear.

"Think Nic will still love you after this one, don't you?"

Harper walked down the hall to where she met Tiana and Saf. She threw her hands over their shoulders ad they began walking down the hallway happily as they discussed.

I looked around me and felt like I was frozen in time.

A hand squeezed my shoulder and I turned around.

It was Nic.

"It's okay Coy, I forgive you, don't wor-." I pushed him to the side and ran down the hall balling my eyes out.

"Coy!" I heard Nic shouting from behind me.

I got my car and it had been covered with toilet paper and eggs. I began pulling all of them off and wiping the windows with my hands.

I unlocked my door and drove off to CVS.

When I got there, I was no longer crying. My eyes were bloodshot red.

I barged into the door and went directly to the supplies aisle and got a box of razors.

I walked to the counter and threw the box of razors onto the counter.

The lady at the counter looked up at me and shook her head in disappointment.

"$4.98," The woman said.

I dropped a 5 dollar bill onto the counter, grabbed the box of razors, which was now in a plastic bag, and left the store.

I got into my car and drove straight home. Thank god, nobodies car was outside the garage, meaning no one was home.

I went into my room and took out the bottle of vodka under my bed. I took a large gulp and took out a razor.

I brought the razor to my wrist and pushed deep and dragged it across my skin.

I was in anguishing pain.

As I continued to cut, blood began dripping onto the floor below me. I couldn't control myself, I could not stop. I went all the way up my wrists and they were pouring with blood.

I grabbed the vodka from my side. This was where the actual pain came to play.

I took a deep breath and began to pour it on my wrists only causing me to cry out in pain and anger.

"Dumbass bitch, you're always fucking up other's lives. Your brothers, your parents, friends, now yourself too. Fuck you, Coy Clent, fuck you!" I shouted as I threw the bottle of vodka to the wall.

My hands were numb and immovable, but it was better this way. In fact, it was amazing this way. The pain is, or at least was, gone.

Chapter 35

It has been one week and I hadn't gone to school once.

My phone was full of messages from Nic. Kingsley sent a few, but there were none from Tia.

"I miss you…" Nic would text.

"I love you, Coy."

"Hey, where are you?"

"Coy, please reply!"

"You did nothing wrong. It's Harper that is going to pay."

A new text message came in from Nic, "I'm coming to get you."

I had showered earlier in the morning but I was dressed in a Panic! At The Disco top and torn jeans.

I heard a knock on the door downstairs then my name being called repeatedly.

"Coy, Coy, Coy?" I could hear Nic shouting from the front yard.

For all he knew, I could be sleeping -- or dead.

I shook off the thought and continues scrolling through all the hate messages I had gotten over the past week.

"I will kill you."

"@stacy61023 she's the one!"

"Backstabbers get hurt!"

"Omfg ew, we were going to be lab partners, God is REAL!"

"@itsbritneybtch oh my god, looks can be deceiving…"

"Kill yourself, whore."

"Boyfriend thief."

"Most bastards are bound to end up like this guys, it's okay."

I heard my front door open and then the person calling my name became louder.

Oh shit, I showed Nic the replica rock with the front door key in it.

"Coy, I'm here for you. Everything is going to be okay." I could hear Nic saying from the outside of my doors.

Tears slid down my cheeks but I quickly wiped
them away.

Nic knocked on the door and began walking in
slowly. He was holding a bag of items in his right
hand and his phone in his left. He came to the foot
of my bed and dropped the bag and his phone.

"Coy, you okay?" He said as he came and sat next
to me.

My eyes began to tear up again, a few trying to slip
away.

I shook my head 'no.'

Nic swooped me up in his arms and held me tight.

"It's okay. You're going to be okay. I don't care
about what they're saying. I only care about you."
Nic whispered in my ear before kissing my
forehead.

"How did you know I was alive?" I said as a tear
slipped down my left cheek.

"You left your messages on 'read'," Nic said.

And for the first time in a good week, I laughed.
Nic joined along too.

"Just promise me you won't do anything stupid,
alright?" Nic held out his pinky to me.

"I promise," I said as I locked pinkies with him.

He got up and got the bag at the foot of the bed. He then walked back to where I was sitting on the bed.

Nic sat down and brought out three items from the bag. A pink and red bear holding a heart, a chocolate box, and apple cider.

"Aw," I said as I cleaned my face and hugged Nic.

"Enough with the sappy moments, let's go to the cheesecake factory," Nic said after moments of holding me.

"Oh my god, are you serious?" I said faintly smiling.
"Absolutely, let's go!" Nic picked me up, lugged me downstairs, and put me in the car.

The whole time I was shouting, "Food, food, cheesecake, cheesecake!"

<u>Chapter 36</u>

I sat in Nic's car as he drove. The Cheesecake
Factory was a distance, but it's the first thing I have
been excited about in a long time.

When Nic picked me up from the bed I praise the
lord the box of chocolates were in my hand. If not, I
would probably die on the way from starvation.
That would be sad, haha.

"So, what do you think you're going to get when we
get there?" Nic said.

"What do you mean?"

Nic let out a small giggle.

"What are you going to ear or try?"

"Everything," I said with a straight face.

"What?" Nic eyes widened before we both burst out
in laughter.

"I'm serious Nic!" I said with a small smirk.

"Well then, we'll just have to see who can eat more
than the other." Nic smiled and then pointed at
himself.

"Hey!" I lightly punched Nic on his arm, "Deal is
on."

As we approached an intersection, Nic turned on the radio.

"Oh, I love this song," I said as I turned up the volume a little bit.

It was an old song by Nelly. I'm pretty sure everyone knows. I began to sing along.

"I said, it's getting hot in here. So take off all your clothes. I am getting so hot, imma take my clothes off..."

Nic's phone buzzed. It was a text message. I turned down the music a little and stopped singing.

"What does it say?" I said to Nic as he picked up his phone in his right hand.

"Oh, it's my mom, I told her we were--," I interrupted.

"Nic..."

"Huh?" Nic continued looking down at his phone.

"Nic," I said again.

"Hold on," he said.

"No, Nic! Look!" I shouted as he looked up from the wheel to see the car.

Nic slammed on the breaks, but by then it was too late.

Everything went black.

Chapter 37

"Charles, the bandages and scissors, stat! This one has got a lot of blood coming out of her upper corner head." A random voice said.

My hands were numb and a mask was over my face. My clothes were drenched in blood, which, by the feels of it, wasn't my own.

I found the strength to move my hand and began to cry and remove the breathing mask.

"No, no, my dear, you're okay, you are in the ambulance." A nurse who noticed my movement said.

"Can you open your eyes sweet pea?" She then said.

I nodded my head and forced my eyes open to be greeted by a bright white light.

"My dear, you had blacked out after being hit," She paused, "You have a minor injury on your head but the doctor has sewn and bandaged it up. In a few minutes, we will arrive at the hospital where you'll rest for a day or two, then your legal guardian may take you home. Do you understand me, dear?"

I told her yes, nodded, then closed my eyes again.

"Where is Nic? The boy who was in the driver's seat." I mumbled weakly through the mask.

"He's okay, he has already made it to the hospital."

I nodded my head and began trying to drift off into sleep. Two minutes past and the movement of the car was becoming sickening.

"Lookie here, we have arrived." The same female nurse whispered as the car came to a stop.

Moments later, the doors of the ambulance were opened and they pulled the stretcher I was on, out, and began rolling me into the hospital.

"Charles, take her to Room 312." The first doctor said.

"Okay," The man I assume was Charles said as he and a few other people took me to 312.

They put me on the bed in the room and told me my food would be up in a few minutes.

The doctors and nurses left the room and shut the door behind them.

I looked around and scanned my surroundings. It was large, with no neighbors, just an empty bed, and curtains over the large windows.
"Nic, where are you?" I said quietly and tilted my head to the right.

The door opened and in came my mother.

"Thank you, Jesus!" She shouted as she ran over to me and gave me a small hug.

"Ow," I said and tried to loosen her grip.

"I'm sorry baby." She said as she wiped the tears on her face and sniffed her nose.

"What happened? How did you end up here? Where is that godd-,"

"Mom, it's okay, I'm okay."

"You sure as hell don't look it," She said as she pointed down at my now bruised body.

"Mom, I'm okay, please it's nobody's fault. But, how did you know I was here, did Dad or Tia-," I coughed a small chunk of blood came out of mouth and fell into my hand. I closed my hand quickly and moved my hand to the corner of the bed before wiping it on a napkin near the bed.

"No, I'm sorry, no reply from either. Tia blocked your number, why is that?" My mom said as she squeezed her face.

Tears threatened to pour down my cheek but I held it in before my mother would know something was up.

"Oh, she did it as a joke, she is going to unblock me later though," I said as I faked a weak smile.

"Mhm, okay. The kids of today and their unexplainable, so-called, jokes."

I turned my head straight causing me to now stare at the ceiling.

"Have you seen Nic?" I asked my mom dully.

"Yes, he's in 313, I believe." My mom said as she took a sear near me and grabbed my hand.

"Oh my god, really? Please let me go and see him! Is he alright? Well obviously he is, isn't he?" I said for the first time in a regular tone.

"Coy."

"Yes, mom?" I smiled faintly.

"You can't go and see Nic, it's not the right time."

"What do you mean? Of course, it is mom. He will think I am avoiding him. I want him, I want to let him know it's not his fault and I don't blame him." I sat up in my bed.

A nurse came inside and placed my food on the desk to the left before exiting the room once again.

"He won't, Coy, he can't be spoken to at the moment. The only people that are allowed to go inside during a time like this is family."

"A time like this?" I squeezed my mouth like a baby, "What do you mean by 'a time like this?'"

I looked at my mother and she had an odd expression on her face.

"Coleen, Nic… Well, he um… He is currently in a coma." My mom said as she squeezed my hand tighter.

"A coma?" I whisper shouted as a few tears slid down my cheeks.

"He well, he is alive, but due to trauma in the accident, his body shut down. He had been in a coma since then." My mom took a deep breath, "But, any day, maybe even today, he could wake up. It's all a matter of time." My mom used her hand and began to wipe the tears that fell from my eyes.

"It's all my fault!" I said as I closed my eyes tight, "Because I was Mrs. Depressed he took me in that car. Now he is suffering the price.

I began to hit myself on the head.

"It's all my fault!" I said again.

My mom restricted me and shouted at me to stop.

"Stop! Coy! It's not your fault!" My mother shouted
as she held me tight.

The tears pouring from my eyes resembled a river. I
loosened myself from my mother's grip and
wrapped my arms around her. I rested my head on
her shoulder and cried the night away.

<u>Chapter 38</u>

I woke up on the left side of my bed to see my mom stretched out on the couch.

It was Tuesday, meaning I could go home. My stay was meant to be 2 days but they extended it to 4 days because of my head injury. It had bled through all of the mumbo jumbo they had put on it.

I tapped the nurse button on the side of my bed and a few seconds later, a nurse named Alana came inside.

"How may I help you?" The nurse said smiling.

"Um, please could we get something to eat? I am feeling a little dizzy," I said pointing at my head.

"Sure, no thing." She said and proceeded to leave the room.

"Thank you!" I semi shouted and sat erect on my bed.

I turned on the TV and turned to my undeniably favorite channel, E!.

They were playing 'I Am Cait,' Rob and Chyna were next. I was very excited because I had never watched Rob and Chyna before, plus, I heard it is a lot of drama.

I upped the television sound, calling my mom to wake up.

"Oh my god, Coy. Why? Do you wish to murder me with the sound of that show?" My mom said as she wiped her eyes.

I laughed and reduced the volume a little.

"Sorry," I said before I continued watching the television show.

My mom went to the bathroom and brushed her teeth. After she was done, I did the same and quickly came back to watch my television.

"Oh, yes, they are finally playing Rob and Chyna," I said as I climbed my hospital bed.

I grabbed the remote and began to turn it up.

"Coleen!" My mother shouted.

I looked at her in the face, rolled my eyes in an exhausted manner, and put the remote back on the corner table.

The nurse came inside with the food and my mouth began to water, "Thank you!" I said as I took the tray.

"And mama Coy," the nurse said as she handed my mom her own tray.

"Thank you," We both said one after the other.

As the nurse was going out, the door was intruded by a frantic nurse.

"Alana! Go to Room 306, the patient who was just moved there is having a stroke!" the nurse said.

Both the nurses ran out quickly and were no longer visible to me.

"Poor person, I hope they're okay." My mother said as she ate the chicken and rice on her plate.

"Right," I said as I watched the television.

My mom got up and dusted her lap off. She placed her tray to the right and began walking towards the door.

"Where are you going, Mom?" I said loudly.

"I'm going down the hall to get a drink," She said as I saw her vanish around the corner.

5 minutes later, she appeared back in front of my room with a Diet Mountain Dew in her hand and a face of concern.

"What's wrong mom?" I said as she approached near my bed.

"Oh, nothing Coy. I lost a dollar, that's all." She
said with a fake smile plastered across her face.

"Mom, stop lying, what is it? Is Nic awake, or?"

The nurse walked into my room prepared to take
away the trays.

"I'm sorry it took me so long to come back! I was
treating a teen boy who was in a reck the other
day." The nurse said.

I pushed my tray to the floor and began to hurl.
What the FUCK.

<u>Chapter 39</u>

It was the day I could finally leave this cursed hospital after two full weeks of almost being here.

My mom was there and she signed all the release forums. Two whole weeks without Nic and there were still no signs of waking up. Well, at least that is what I've been told, and what they have been telling me has not been the truth.

My mom paid the overly expensive bill and we left the hospital.

We walked to the car all the way in the back of the parking lot.

"Mom, are you sure there are no more updates on Nic?" I questioned as I opened up the back door to the car.

"Well, I'm not sure Coy. I haven't been able to talk to his folks, I've only been able to walk passed his room," she said in a tired yet annoyed way.

I left it at that and sat down in the car. She started the car and we drove off.

When we arrived home and walked inside the door, I was surprised at what I had seen; Harper.

I dropped my shoes and ran up the stairs to my room and shut the door behind me.

What does she want from me now?

"Coy, you have a visitor! And that is no way to treat them." I heard my mom shout from downstairs followed by footsteps on the stairs.

I went to the door to close and lock it but it was too late, Harper had made her entrance.

"Hey, Coin," Harper said as she stepped inside my room and closed the door behind her.

"Wha-a-t do you want?" I stuttered.

Harper let out a laugh and looked down and back up at me.

"So after all of the shit you've gone through, you're still scared of me?"

I rolled my eyes and took a step back.

"Well anyway, now that you're okay or whatever, let me tell you; When Nic wakes up, you and him are over. When you return to school, no mention of what happened, and if anyone asks you, keep your mouth shut. I do not want or need to handle another mess made by you."

Harper blew a kiss at me and exited my room. To cover up her tracks she shouted, "I love you Coy," As she went down the stairs and left the house.

I went to my bed, fell forward, and began to sob into my pillow.

When would Nic come back to me? How long will I have to suffer in silence at the hands of Harper? Why am I even here anymore?

All the thoughts that ran through my head were frightening. Some though were causing me pain.

Maybe I really shouldn't be here.

Chapter 40

It had been four months and there was no news about the current state of Nic. Switching to online school was the best decision I had made so far, but I still found it hard to grasp onto the concept of life after everything I had been through.

It was 1 in the afternoon and no one was home but me. I went into the bathroom and took a deep look into the mirror. There was a large scar on my head from the glass that cut me during the accident.

I used the toilet, washed my hands, and face in the sink, then brushed my teeth. Before I turned on the shower, I heard my phone ringing. It was probably my mom.

I walked to my room and as I guessed, it was my mom. I picked up my phone and clicked the green button that picked the call.

"Hello?" I said on the phone.

"Hello baby, are you okay? Has anyone called you yet?" My mom said on the other side of the line, her voice shaky.

"Called me? About what?" I said sounding confused.

"It's fine, I will tell you when I get home in a little while."

"No, Mom. Tell me what happened, now. I don't
have that patience. Is it about Dad, you? Nic?"

My mom took a deep breath and I heard her sniffle
through the phone.

"Coy, he's brain dead." My mom said. At this point,
she was crying.

"Who, mom? Who?"

My mom continued crying on the phone.

"Nicholas!" She said briefly and cried even harder.

The phone fell out of my hand and I went numb.

I couldn't feel anything, I couldn't hear anything,
my vision was blurry. I could not cry, I had nothing
left in me. This was the last straw.

I walked downstairs and opened up the medicine
drawer and grabbed every pill bottle in sight.

I sat down on the couch in my house and took in my
surroundings.

"Well, this it is," I said as I chuckled to myself.

"You won. You FUCKING WON!" I screamed out
to nobody as I opened all the caps of the pill bottles.

I poured it all out on the counter, stood up, and looked for a piece of paper and a pen, and began to write my letter.

Hey Mom,
Just know, that there was nothing you could do to stop this. At this point, it was a long time coming, and if you haven't noticed it, well this might take you by surprise. I ended it because, I felt my time was up. My spirit is broken and I can't heal it, trust me, I've tried. I love you SO much. Remember me for everything I was, not what I am now. I will always be your little girl, and I will always be with you. Nic was the last thing I had, the only friend I had. At least this way, I will see him.

Till We Meet Again,
Your Daughter, Coy

I folded the letter and left it where I knew she would see it; her bed. I walked back to the couch with tears in my eyes, sat down, and downed over 100 pills.

After 39 minutes, my vision started blurring and I could see a white light.

"I'm sorry God. I am so sorry. Please forgive me." I said as a faint smile appeared on my face.

I was finally going home, I would be in peace.

At 2:13 pm on July 17th, 2019, I died on my living room floor.

<u>Chapter 41</u>

My eyes were blinking and I could see a bright light and lots of sounds that I could not register.

"Help! He is awake! My baby is waking up!" I heard a drowned-out voice say.

I was still trying to see what was going on.

"Nicholas? If you can register what is happening, please blink twice." A man I believed to be a doctor said.

I blinked my eyes twice.

"Please open up your mouth." The doctor said and I did so.

He clicked his flashlight and told the nurses and my parents I was okay.

Two hours later and I was finally able to fully open my eyes. I looked around me and saw my parents faces flushed red and with tears. But, they were happy to see me.

My mom came up to me and gave me the largest hug, but it hurt like hell. I guess my body was still sore.

"What day is it?" I asked my mom.

"Nicholas, that doesn't matter at the moment." She
said.

"Please, tell me the date mom," I said in a weeping
voice.

"It's July 23rd, 2019." She said in a sad tone and
she touched my arm.

"I've been out for almost 5 months? Where is
Coy?" I said in a shaky tone.

My mom kept silent.

"Where is Coy, mom!" I said in a sad voice.

"She's gone baby, she's gone." My mom said.

Tears fell down my face. It was my fault. I wasn't
there for her, and now, I could never be.